IF IT S NOT LOVE

LOVE

Syed Arshad

HESTEN
An imprint of BlueRose Publishers

First Published in 2013
Revised edition in 2018

ISBN: 978-93-88184-47-2
Price: INR 100/-

H E S T E N
An imprint of BlueRose Publishers

www.bluerosepublishers.com
info@bluerosepublishers.com
+91 8882 898 898

Cover Design:
Khhyati Mittal

Typographic Design:
Saakshi Kaushal

Distributed by: Blue Rose, Amazon, Flipkart, Shopclues

Dedicated to

My parents

Kakuli ma'am (you are the best teacher ever!)

Prof. Razi Ahmad (thank you uncle, for everything)

All my friends

And last but not the least…

the person who shared his true story, which formed

the basis of this fiction.

The melting sun was still shining bright; but brighter was his face with gaiety and excitement. He stepped out of the taxi. A few hundred metres away, stood erect the nation's pride, 'The India Gate.' His prolonged stare at his most desired place in the world, for at least the last 25 years, made his eyes moist and a smile dilate at the same time.

"Sir... sir", the taxi driver called him out twice from inside the cab, but on getting no response, she stretched her hand out of the window and patted on his wrist. "Mr. Khanna", she said softly. "Ye...yes", he replied confused, as if shaken awake from a dream. The driver had a pen and a small receipt in her hand. "Sir, you need to sign here and write the online pay code you got for booking this taxi," she said with a mild smile on her face. "Oh! Of course," he smiled back. Taking the receipt, he penned down the formalities and returned it. "Is that okay?" He looked at her for assurance. She took a glimpse at the paper and nodded, "Yes sir," she said with a smile. A bigger one this time.

"Any martyr in the family?" she asked very casually while keeping the receipt in her pocket. "Why do you ask?" The question surprised him. She shrugged slightly, "Never seen anybody with such complicated expressions here, before." She was looking at the monument while saying the last four words. He followed her gaze and then let out a small chuckle. "Oh no! A completely different story, I'm here to see someone." The laugh shrank to a thought-lost gentle smile as he continued, "someone I haven't seen in 25 years, someone I missed every single day for all these years, someone who promised me an hour of her life, this evening, here, someone whose promise has been the sole reason of..." his eyes met hers. He stopped for a while, looking straight into those wide open, eager, and questioning eyes and then completed his sentence, "...my existence." She kept staring at him, surprised to the core. "Wow!" was all she said after a couple of seconds. He smiled, "Take care child", he patted her head, turned and headed down the road to The Gate.

"Hats off, what a love Sir," she shouted as he walked towards his spot. He turned around to face her and said loudly, "You are mistaken", and smiled softly, "it's not love."

IF IT S NOT
LOVE

He jumped off the last three stairs in a hurry to catch the about-to-leave metro. His silky black hair fell on to his glittering brownish eyes. Holding his bag with his left hand and pulling the hair back with the right one, he ran towards the open doors of the very first coach, right in front; the 'Ladies only'. This might get me into trouble, but not the kind if I miss the train, he thought. A little scared, a little excited, Aarav ventured his way through. The moment he entered the coach, the doors started to close. He looked at the closing doors, turned his face away and then closed his eyes in relief, as if it was not five minutes but five hours that he had saved.

"You are in the wrong compartment my son", a thick feminine voice hit his eardrum. He opened his eyes to look for the sonorous source. A lady in her fifties with a feigned smile was looking at him. "Actually aunty", he tried to come up with an explanation that would convey his desperation in shoving himself into the wrong compartment, but the words froze in his mouth as the lady continued with her annoyed expression and as an add on, was pointing her finger towards the other end of the compartment. The message was clear, Get out! No explanation! Being left with no other option, he started moving towards the rear end of the compartment. "Excuse me, excuse me", squeezing his way through some angry looks, trying to make his way out ASAP when his phone rang. He took it out of his pocket, hoping the call was worth picking up in that mess. He looked at the display, then out of a window pane. The train was still running underground. Fearing bad connection, he disconnected the call and picked a place to stand, right across the 'no man's land!'

The sweat drops on his forehead and the rest of his tensed face were shouting out loud, narrating the rush he had been through that chilly morning. He was continuously switching his gaze from his cell phone's display to the window pane, while waiting for the sunlight, or more precisely, the connection. *Next stop Hauz Khas.* Upon listening to the announcement, he looked at the direction chart, *God! 11 more stations!* He exclaimed to himself. He looked at his cell's display again to see the time, but to his surprise found the signal bars on the screen, appearing one by one. *This is just enough*, he said to himself and dialed the last missed call. "Ya hi ma'am, this is Aarav here", perhaps the person on the other end was not able to recognize him, or the connection was still bad, so a second later he spoke a little louder,

"Aarav Khanna here". On getting a positive response, he continued, "ya I might be a little late, it will take me around thirty more minutes to reach, is that okay?" By looking at the relief on his face anybody in the world could have guessed the answer was a yes from the other end.

"Interview", he said smilingly, after disconnecting the call, to a stout guy in front of him who seemed absorbed in Aarav's HTC, more than his conversation. He gave a fake smile and got busy with his Nokia. Gauging his disinclination, Aarav, while taking a glimpse at the direction chart again, pulled out his hands-free from his bag, connected it to his cell phone and plugged in the buds in his ears to listen to some of his favorite tracks.

Ummm... she's good but a little too tall, next, wow beautiful eyes but seems like a bookworm kinzz. Listening to the music and checking out the best figures from the whole bunch of ladies out front was one of his favourite past time. *Oh God! too big to handle!* He exclaimed inside. With raised brows and forced breath he moved onto next, to next, and after scanning almost the whole of the compartment and getting the same greedy looks from a few in return, he smiled sheepishly to himself and got busy changing the track. *Too much of English songs since morning.* He pressed the stop key on Katy Perry and started looking for Sonu Nigam.

While he was into playlist penetration, he heard a suppressed laugh. His eyes closed automatically as if he had heard a thousand pearls scattering. His heartbeat increased a little. He opened his eyes and searched for the source of his interest. He saw a girl standing beside the first door of the ladies coach, same side as his, talking over her cell phone. With her back towards him he could barely see her face. He bent his neck as much as he could and got a partial glance of the shades-covered face. *How could you miss this?* He said to himself, *seems like she is as beautiful as her voice.* He diverted his entire attention towards her, to see a little more, to hear a little more, but apart from a few words of hers, he couldn't hear much. *There is something different about her, something so fresh, so appealing,* he thought. "Arjangarh station", the computerized voice announced. The train slowed down to a halt and as the doors were about to open, she turned her face towards him and gave a smile, perhaps the world's most beautiful one; atleast for Aarav at that moment; and deboarded the train.

Was that for me? He looked around, *seems like!* he thought, on finding no other contender. *Shall I get down? But my interview? Oh God! Those shades, I'm not even sure, but if that was for me, I'm losing a jackpot here, shall I give it a traaa...* he pulled his step back. He hadn't even completed the sentence in his mind when the doors closed, on his train as well as his thoughts.

***

TEN DAYS LATER

"Any questions?" Himanshu asked in his unique Indo-American accent, while looking into his laptop. The whole batch was quiet or maybe tired. He raised his head, his specs a little lower on his nose, and he looked through the whole batch, "guess it's a no", he said sportily while turning off his laptop. "All right guys that's all from my end for now, Miss Anjali will take it from here", he announced, keeping his specs in the case. At the back row, Aarav pinched Neil on his thigh. "Ouch!!" Neil cried, "are you mad?" He murmured. "Miss Anjali", Aarav rustled back, mischievously.

"Any problem?" Himanshu asked with a designed smile on his face. Neil returned the smile, but an embarrassed one; "no", he shook his head slightly. "Suddenly the class seems to has awakened", Himanshu said, as he walked across the training room to step out. He still

had the same expressions but that intonation made everyone burst into laughter. "Guys, the next session will start in a while, so you can take a 20 minute break". By now, he had reached the door. He pulled it open and turned towards the batch, "remember guys, 20 minutes means 20 minutes", he cautioned, while tapping his wrist watch with his forefinger, like everytime and walked out.

"Let's go", Aarav stood up and said casually to Neil, who was still inflamed.

"You are an asshole", he said with a sheepish grin and stood up to join him.

"I know that, but man she is just so hot, can't control my emotions", Aarav was laughing and with the same stupid countenance, tried to hug him.

"Stay away", Neil hit his stomach with his elbow.

"Ouch!!" with one hand on his stomach Aarav managed to put the other one around Neil's shoulder, "come on Hunter let's go for a *sutta*", he said and dragged him out.

The slow sound of radio compounded with intermittent dog barks in the midst of the night, was what gave that place a unique touch. Most of the people preferred going to the sophisticated cafeteria upstairs, but for the smokers, this was the most relaxing place. Though a little unhygienic, the menu comprised of everything; eateries, cold drinks, juices, tea and of course one extra item, *sutta* (cigarettes), all in one, "jitte da dhaba"; no less than a superstore.

"Wanna have something to eat?" Neil jerked his brows, while looking at Aarav.

"No", Aarav replied making a face and shook his head. Neil turned towards the shopkeeper and placed his order, "two malboro lights and two tea." Next minute, both of them had tea in one hand and the silent killer in another.

"The night's too cold man", Neil said as they were looking for a place to sit. "There", Aarav pointed at a dingy bench. "Aah, that's so dirty", Neil cringed. Aarav stared at him for a couple of seconds, walked upto the bench and settled himself, a minute later Neil joined him.

"You understood that call disposition part?" Aarav asked, while looking into his tea cup and letting the smoke out through his mouth and nose.

"Ya almost, it was easy", Neil replied and looked towards Aarav, who had an 'Oh-Really!' expression on his face. "Yaar, it's not as complicated as it seems to be", Neil tried to justify, "you just need to memorise the abbreviations, and it's gonna be simple". Aarav said nothing, but raised the middle finger of the hand he was holding his tea cup with.

"Behanchoo", Neil said slowly, and put his sutta between his lips.

"Anjali is hot, isn't she?" wanting to be involved in a rather more meaningful conversation, Aarav said, while taking a sip of his tea.

"Ya too bloody hot", Neil replied with a fancied sigh, looking at his half finished *sutta*. "Do you think she has a boyfriend?" he turned his face towards Aarav.

"How would I know?"

"Hmmm..."

"Why don't you try, seems to me she is interested in you", knowing it's a lie, Aarav managed a serious note, trying his best to control his laughter.

"Aah! I wish I could", with a deep breath Neil said, "you know na, Sakshi loves me so much, I can't betray her yaar", he explained his helplessness and went silent for a while, but returned aggressively, "saale tu kyu nai karta try", he said in his typical Guwahati accent, slow Hindi.

"I'm not sure if she has a boyfriend, once I get to know the truth, I'll apply", knowing that Neil must have had a big question mark expression on, Aarav turned his face towards him and clarified, "you know anybody can sit on a vacant chair", he paused with a foxy smile on his face, "but that doesn't match Aarav Khanna's profile." Finishing the last puff, he threw it in style.

"Behanchoo."

"When are we gonna hit the floor to make our fortune?" Neil added after a brief silence.

"Lets see, today is February 24,", after a couple seconds calculation, Aarav added, "within ten days, that is by 5 March, you and I will be on the floor taking calls", he said rather loudly and then sighed, "provided we clear the damn assessment, and Sir, keep this in mind, making incentives here is not that easy", he said wriggling his finger.

"Ya whatever", Neil shrugged slightly, "but this company is really good; nice cabs, such good trainers, shorter shifts and of course, so many hot chicks", Neil threw light on the positive sides, "it's been just two weeks and I have met so many people who are making good money".

"Let's see", Aarav stood up, and pulled out his HTC, "it's already 15 minutes".

"Really?"

As they were about to enter the company's premises, Neil turned his face towards Aarav, "tomorrow and day after are our week-offs, wanna come over and see me and my band jamming", even before Neil was done with his proposal, Aarav shook his head, "your place is too far man and I don't think I'll be able to take out time from boozing", smilingly, Aarav justified his 'no'. "Next time for sure", he said and wrapped his arm around Neil's shoulder.

"Behanchoo."

***

"So, you have to understand the mood and portrait of the consumer, like for example if the consumer is irate, let him vent, let him speak, listen to his problems and then proceed with the call as smartly as you can", she stopped and swayed her eyes through the batch, "remember guys, smartness is the first factor for being a good collector", she paused, "of course, hard work is the second but equally important", she completed with a smile. High heels, snug fit jeans, paired with a short denim shirt, pretty Miss Anjali was addressing the trainees. "I need you to jot down these important points of today's topic, "Situation Handling", picking up the marker from the table, she turned towards the white board.

"Wow!" Neil pressed Aarav's hand, "she looks so hot in casuals, thank god it's Friday", he added with a faint sigh. "Sakshi", Aarav said slowly in his ears and smiled at the transition in Neil's expression from wow to sorry. "Go on Rocco, she is all your's", Neil surrendered. "Ghnnnn…ghnnnn", Aarav was still smiling when he felt his cell phone vibrate, he took it out from his pocket, "Anup bhaiya", the display said and his smile vanished like smoke in thin air.

"Anjali", he stood up. She turned around, "yes Aarav?" her eyes widened a little.

"I'm getting this important call, do you mind if I..." with the cell phone in his hand, he pointed towards the door.

"Oh! Sure, go ahead", she smiled.

"Who is it?" Neil murmured.

"Brother", Aarav replied and walked out of the training room.

***

"Hello", Aarav said, standing beside the fountain at the back of the office.

"Hey, my brother, I thought you are sleeping, I was about to disconnect, how are you?" A coarse voice answered.

"I'm fine", Aarav replied blandly, "how're things at home?"

"How do you expect it to be, without you. It's been like a year now, come back", Anup stumbled through the words.

"Bhaiya, it's one in the night and you seem drunk, we'll talk later", Aarav tried to avoid the conversation.

"I'm drunk, but you have lost your consciousness, any idea how embarrassing all this is for dad?" He shouted.

"I'll come back, but not now", Aarav said in the same lifeless tone.

"Go to hell," came the reply after a moment and the line got disconnected. Aarav kept looking at the phone for a while. He pressed his temples, raising his face towards the sky, and closed his eyes to relax himself. "Ghnnnn… ghnnnn", he felt the vibration, *Oh! Not again*, he said and looked down at his cell with half opened eyes. *Mandy*, it said and his eyes regained the normal radius. *Why at this time?* He thought and received the call, "Hey Mandy."

"Thank god man you're awake", sighed the person on the other end.

"It's been a long time, how are you, everything's alright?" Aarav seemed surprised at his call at such odd hour.

"Ya just a little busy with the job hunt, you know", he desisted, "actually yaar I … aa…I need some money", he completed, fumblingly.

"Ya sure how much, and when?"

"Yaar sister is serious, dad just called, I need to go home now".

"Now?"

"Ya, if you could lend me the money, I'll take the morning flight".

"Okay, how much do you need?"

"Umm… fifteen thousand, possible?"

"Ya", he confirmed, after a crisp calculation. "Shall I come down to the airport directly, I'm in Gurgaon right now", he added.

"Yaar I know I'm asking too much, but is it like possible for you to come down to my place, I haven't paid my rent for the last two months. On seeing a lock, my landlord is gonna create a scene in the morning letting the entire neighbourhood know and if I tell him now, he won't let me go", Mandy said.

"Alright, not a problem, so you're still in the same flat?"

"No, another one, in Chitranjan Park, near Govindpuri."

"Okay, I'll call you once I reach there, I'm at work, will leave at two."

"Thanks yaar."

"Pack your bags, see you in a while."

***

"I won't go this side", the driver said firmly, stopping the cab at a red light, half a kilometer away from Aaarv's destination. Aarav glared at him for a while and stepped out. *This is the price that you have to pay on getting aligned in another cab*, he thought, left the cab and started walking down the road.

February end is not usually this cold, God knows what's wrong this year! He thought looking at the fog around. *It's freezing!* He mumbled while he put on his jacket's hood over his head and pulled his muffler up his nose; hands inside his jeans front pocket. After a ten minute walk, he pulled out his cell to call Mandy, to make sure he was going the right way. "Meow ...meow", a quelled kitten cry caught his attention just as he was about to dial. He stopped and turned his head around.

"Meow... meow" The second cry helped him gauge the fount. He walked back a few steps, looked down and saw a densely furred snow white kitten stuck under a fence along the footpath. "Oou! You're stuck", he interjected. She looked up at him. Her innocent eyes pleading for help. He stooped, held her gently and tried to pull her out. "Meow meow!" she cried out louder. He bent a little more and with his cell phone's light saw a little blood on her back. He moved the light up her back on the fence; there was a nail. "Oh god!" he felt pity, "let me get you out another way", he touched the ground below her, it was all mud. He started digging it out to make some space but in the cold weather his hands were not working with the expected pace. He looked around for something that could be used as a tool at that moment. A little ahead on the road he saw a wooden piece. He ran to grab it and as he returned, he saw someone completely covered in a thin blanket, with only the eyes undraped, on the other side of the fence. "Aaaa!" the person exclaimed in a low pitch and fell back on seeing Aarav, who, being terrified himself, moved a few steps back. Only on realizing by the voice that it was a living human, and that too a girl, did he pull himself together. "Sorry I didn't mean to scare you", he looked into her eyes, which were not clearly visible in that foggy dark night, "just trying to help", he said, switching his eyesight to the kitten. She kept looking at him for a few seconds but said nothing and then grabbed the kitten from her end and tried to pull. "No, no, no!" Aarav almost shouted. "Shhhhhh!" she hushed, putting her finger on the blanket covered lips. "Sorry", he said slowly and bent down on his knees, "look", he lighted up his cell phone to show her the cut and the nail. "God!" Pain reflected in her voice.

"Hold on", Aarav said and started digging with the wooden piece. After a ten minute struggle, he managed to dig enough to pull the kitten out. She held the kitty and started to pull gently. Aarav tried to give her a hand from his end and in the attempt his finger touched hers, she flinched and looked into his eyes. The kitten was safe in her hands but they both kept looking at each other for a few seconds and then suddenly, she stood up and ran back. Aarav saw her disappear in the fog.

"Who are you?" he asked the receding figure slowly, being mysteriously touched.

As he was about to rise, his gaze fell onto a glittering object on the other side of the fence. He stretched his hand to grab it. It was a silver bracelet. He thought of calling after her, but there was no sign of her. He stood up and examined it, bringing it a little closer to his eyes. It was a beautiful piece of work and attached to it with a thin small chain, something was hanging. *Probably a name!* He thought. The language was alien to him. *I'll come back here someday and return it,* thinking this, he kept it in the inner pocket of his jacket. "What place is it, anyway?" He looked up for a sign board, but couldn't find one. He frowned with disappointment, shrugged slightly and moved ahead.

***

"I'm near Agarwal Sweets", he called up Mandy.

"Just walk a little ahead and take left, you'll be able to see me", Mandy replied.

"Alright", he hung up.

He took the left turn and saw Mandy standing on the road with his bags. "Hey man, you look like a terrorist", he said, pointing towards

Aarav's hood and muffler as he gave a half hug in a typical boyish style. Just then Aarav realized why that girl had gotten scared. He smiled.

"All set?" looking at the bags, Aarav asked.

"Ya, I've called a cab. It should be here any moment. I had some cash so I cleared some of my dues with my landlord, luckily he agreed to settle it at half my expectation", he said in a single breath, "sorry I made you come this far".

"No problem, I got dropped by office cab", Aarav fished out his wallet, "here's the money, and can you drop me?"

"Ya sure", Mandy said while keeping the money in his wallet.

"What's that place, with fences around?" Aarav asked.

"Where?" Mandy looked at him.

"That side", Aarav pointed to his back.

"No idea, I seldom go that side", with bent lips Mandy replied.

"That's our cab, I guess", Aarav said, looking at an approaching car behind Mandy.

"Green park first and then airport, okay?" Mandy said to the cab driver as they got inside the cab.

***

"Ghnnnn... ghnnn", the strong vibration of his phone woke him up. Aarav sank deeper into the pillow to avoid it, but as it continued bothering, he raised his head and with a half-opened eye, looked at the wall clock which said 11:20 A.M. "God! Who the hell is it so early on a Saturday morning?" He hunted out his cell phone from under the quilt. 'Shayna', the display said. "Oou no!" he hit his forehead with his palm and a second later received the call.
"Hii shay."

"Hii sexy, where are you, it's my day off, coming to see you", a sugary voice replied.

"Aaaa... me? Ummm... I'm at a friend's place."

"And you forgot to put the lock on?"

"What?"

"I'm standing right outside your door, you liar".

He opened the door. High heels, salwar suit, bangles, earrings, hair tied back with a few strands down on the beautiful face, Shayna was staring at him angrily. "You look cute when you are mad", shorts-clad Aarav tried to pacify her, while wiping the corner of his eye. "And you look like a dirty rat when you lie, put your shirt on", she invaded, pushing him aside.

"What a mess!" she clamored, with both her hands on her waist.

"What mess, everything's placed perfectly where it's supposed to be", he fell on his bed again, face down.

"Ya I can see, shoes nicely placed on the chair, towel on the monitor, clothes on the sofa, and wow, ash tray on your oh-so-clean bed. Perfect!"

"Take it easy yaar, you must be tired, come on", he patted the bed twice with his palm.

As she was walking upto the bed, Aarav pointed his finger towards the kitchen, "grab a bottle of water please".

"You're impossible", she turned towards the kitchen. "You should be the one getting me water", she shouted out from inside the kitchen, while opening the refrigerator door.

"What is this?" she was back in the room, holding a bottle of water in one hand and a bowl with some noodles in it, in the other.

"What?" he raised his head a little and looked at the bowl, "Oh! That's Chow Chow, Nepali noodles, a friend gave it to me", he smiled and downed his head back in the bed.

"This looks horrible. You had this for dinner yesterday?"

"Yesterday, I was at work, came back at around four in the morning, so you can call it breakfast".

"Work?" she was dumping the noodles in the dustbin, "a call centre again?"

"Hmmm...Midllan, you must have heard its name".

"No, I haven't", she sounded infuriated.

"It's a collection company, one of the largest in the United States, they offer good incentives along with..."

"You're spoiling your life", she didn't let him complete.

"I'm not in the mood for another lecture session, had enough in the training yesterday", he almost shouted at her. She went silent. "Where am I supposed to pay my rent and other bills from?"

"I have been laid off for the last two months", he added after a while, but the pitch was a little lower. She kept the bottle on the table, walked upto the bed, laid down beside him and put her soft hand on his face.

"My Aaru is angry?" she said, tangling her fingers in his thick silky hair, "Look, you're a fashion designer from NIFT. If you don't like assisting someone, join your family business or may be together we can set up our own," she moved closer and added, "but a call centre?"

"Don't come this close Shay", he brought his lips close to hers, "what if I lose control?"

She looked at his lips, then into his eyes, "I'm dying for that day", she said naughtily. He smiled and kissed her forehead. "I'll go freshen up", he got down from the bed and looked around for his towel.

"But seems to me like you don't want to lose it", she was still lying on the bed with her eyes closed.

"Where is my towel?" He tried to ignore.

"On the monitor Sir", she said. He picked it up, put it on his shoulder and headed towards the bathroom. "Everything's placed perfectly where it's supposed to be", she imitated his tone and without looking at his reaction, got down from the bed and started cleaning up.
"Shay do it properly", he couldn't control his laughter, after keeping a serious note through the sentence. She turned towards him to give a dirty look but he had already stepped inside the bathroom by then.

"And make it fast Mr. Properly. We'll go for lunch and then for a movie", she said loudly, with a smile on her face.

"Lunch is okay, but movie? I'm afraid I gotta go to work", he replied even louder from inside the bathroom, after a while.

She said nothing but glared furiously at the bathroom door.

***

"One dal makhani and one karhai paneer with plain butter naan", he returned the menu to the waiter with a smile.

"Couldn't you find a better place?" She looked around in disdain.

"Can't afford Taj now", he smiled.

"Aarav, what is it that you are trying to prove?"

"That this place is no less than Taj", he said looking around, "a little compromised on the infra part though", he smirked.

"That wasn't funny."

"Wanna have a cold drink?" he turned his face to call a waiter. But before he could, she kept her hand on his, "Aaru, I want you to talk to your father, maybe he was angry when he said you are nothing without him. It's already been a year now. Being your girlfriend, I feel so bad about you living this way. Just think what your father must be going through".

"Hmmm…"

"Aarav, there's nothing to be ashamed about calling your father and saying sorry."

"All right", he stretched it, to signal a stop. "So how is your on-job training going, enjoying assisting that bitch?" He added, clearly to change the topic.

"She is opening a new outlet."

"Really! Must have got a little more arrogant then."

"Yaa…" she said, making a face, "at times I feel like you did the right thing leaving that humiliating place."

"Why don't you do that then?"

"Just learning the fashion industry's business ethics, hoping to use them against her some day", she smiled wickedly.

"Sir, here's your paneer, dal and naan", the waiter said while placing them on the table.

"Thank you and two cokes please."

"Smells good", he said while rubbing his palms together.

"Won't you get fixed offs here? And what did you say the name of the company is?" she asked while picking a naan from the basket.

"Midllan…and the offs won't usually be on weekends. During the training, it's just on Sundays."

"It's the last Sunday of the month tomorrow. I'll be working, Aaru. Take a day off today please", she made a cute face.

He smiled and slightly shook his head, "Can't. Not during the training atleast. Himanshu and Anjali, my trainers, are very strict about leaves. They will ask a million questions, and still not approve it."

He looked at the meal and asked, "Anything else?"

"No", she said and twisted her lips sideways, in a typical girlish vogue.

"Let's go to Select City mall, we'll have an icecream there", gauging her displeasure, he tried to bribe her. She smiled.

It worked, like always.

***

"I'm gonna get my favourite", she chirped as they reached the Baskin Robbin's outlet, "and you?" she turned towards Aarav.

"I've got this", he showed his cigarette packet to her.

While they were walking down the lane, relishing their own distinctive flavors, somebody shouted out his name from behind. They turned around, and Aarav was surprised to see Neil running towards him.

"God! Where did he appear from? It's gonna be a mess today", Aarav said to himself.

"Hey man, yesterday you said…" Neil was panting from his sprint. "Neil, my brother", Aarav hugged him, "don't utter a word, just keep your mouth shut", he whispered in his ear.

"This is Shayna, my grandmother", he said sarcastically. She hit him on his shoulder, "His girlfriend. Hii, and you?"

"Neil", he answered, without a smile, as he was asked not to utter a word. He wore a confused expression. Aarav held him by putting an arm around his shoulder, "pura naam bata."

"Neilutpal Bhuchiyan", Aarav answered himself before Neil could open his mouth. "My two weeks old, but a really good friend, struggling musician, lead vocalist of a band named 'Stringzz attached' and my colleague at Midllan". Shayna raised her brows, "Really?"

"Ya... and I was actually planning to go to his place after getting you an auto, he lives nearby."

"What for?" She interrogated.

"To get myself aligned in his cab, a simple saving of hundred bucks", he replied smartly. She kept looking at him for a couple of seconds, "Fine, get me an auto then", she turned and started walking towards the main road. Aarav and Neil followed.

"What's going on?" Neil muttered. Aarav pulled the virtual lip zip and placed his forefinger on his lips, beckoning silence.

"Text me after getting the cab, and after reaching the office as well and call me during your breaks", she boarded an auto. "That's why I said she is my grandmother", Aarav said to Neil, with a smile, while handing over two crisp hundred rupee notes to the auto driver. She hit him on his shoulder, "and no chow chow kinds, proper dinner, okay", she held his hand with a little tear in her eyes and was still trying to smile, "take care" she said slowly. "Bye" Aarav patted her cheeks. "Bye Neil", wiping her tears with one hand; she waved the other one to Neil. The auto started and in a blink of an eye, disappeared in the traffic.

They were still standing at that place. Aarav took out his packet of cigarette, "*sutta*?" and offered one to Neil.

"Tea first."

Aarav kept it back in his pocket and they looked around for a roadside tea stall. "There", Neil found one and they started walking towards it.

"Why did you lie to your girlfriend, that we are going to office?"

"Girlfriend is what she claims to be, but I don't love her and as far as lying is concerned, I have to booze and she wanted me to spend the entire evening with her".

"You lie like a gas –meter", Neil laughed.

"Not even a single drop of beer for a week now", Aarav sounded serious, "You stay close? Let's go booze at your place, if you or your roommate doesn't have any problem"

"My band's guitarist is my room mate, he went to his friend's place after the jamming session", Neil looked angrily towards him, "that's why I asked you to come over, but it was too far for you until yesterday and saale, aaj icecream khane pahoch gaya".

Aarav shrugged, "gas-meter", he said with a wicked smiled.

"Behanchoo."

***

"Enough", Neil shouted, as Aarav poured some more beer in his glass.

"Life's pear, with bloody beer", quite drunk, Aarav poured the left over in his own glass.

"Who said that, Albert Einstein?"

"Nopes, Aarav Khanna", he burped.

"That's why it stinks".

"Saale, it's your wash starved bed sheet and socks that stink", Aarav gulped his fifth drink bottoms-up and plonked the glass on the floor. "Oye chips all finished", he kicked Neil, who was busy lighting another cigarette. Neil looked at the empty packets of snacks, then at Aarav, who, pointed towards the kitchen door.

"Hell man, you eat too fast, let me see if I have got something back in there", Neil heaved himself up and with uneven steps, walked into the kitchen.

"What is it?" Aarav shouted.

"Eggs," pat came the reply, in the same pitch.

"Great", Aarav said slowly, leaning against the bed with his eyes closed.

"Tin... tin", the Message tone made him open his eyes. On seeing Neil's phone display light up, he bent forward to pick it up. "That's mine", Neil came running from the kitchen and almost snatched it from him.

"When did I say it's mine?" Aarav pulled his hand back and resumed his pose. "Who is it?" he asked, on seeing Neil smiling into his cell.

"Sakshi! She has changed her profile picture on FB and wants me to like it", Neil said.

"Hey I haven't seen her yet. Have you got internet connection, need to check my messages as well".

"Why? Don't you have it in your HTC?"

"Aaaa... no, it keeps you occupied all the time and moreover I'm not that 24*7 online kind of a person."

"Asshole", Neil said and walked upto his computer, "why don't you keep a cell phone like mine then?" He added while turning it on.

"Something's burning man", Aarav said. Neil nodded in agreement. They rotated their heads, sniffing, to find the source, looked towards each other and a second later, shouted at the top of their voices, "it's the egg!!" They ran towards the kitchen.

"It's no longer eatable, almost burnt", looking at the frying pan in Aarav's hand, Neil said sadly.

Aarav put it on the floor, settled down and raised a beer bottle like a trophy, "everything's bearable with beer", he laughed and put a small piece of the burnt egg in his mouth, "umm it's good, now c'mon show me the picture of the lady who got our omlette burnt". Neil made a face, on seeing him eating that. He turned towards the computer and got busy with it.

"The computer will take a few minutes to start", Neil said and sat on the floor to join him.

"So how did you two meet?" Aarav asked, pouring some beer in his glass.

"We know each other since childhood, grew up in the same locality, studied in the same school, I proposed to her when we were in class 9th, she accepted and we are together since then", he took a sip of his drink and added, "you know what, she is the only person apart from my mother who supports my passion for music. She believes in me", he went a little slow with the last sentence, staring into distance and a second later gulped the whole glass in a go, "she is twenty-five hundred kilometers away, back in Guwahati, but I can always feel her presence with me", he smiled.

"You're lucky. You got two important people in your life to support you", Aarav smiled back.

"Why, your mother doesn't support you?"

"She died when I was ten."

"Hey, what's with Shayna?" Neil's expression said he felt sorry about Aarav's mother, but he asked this a little later, perhaps to avoid the awkward situation.

"Nothing. We were in the same college, but different batches. One fine morning she proposed to me, I never said 'yes', but still, we are together since then", Aarav said.

Neil raised his brows, "So it's just fun for you ha?" He said with a foxy smile.

"No yaar, not with her."

"Why?"

Aarav shrugged slightly, "I've got my own little principles around this, either it should be fun both ends or love both ends."

"But seems like she loves you a lot and moreover man, she is hot", drunk to his guts, Neil laughed out loud, pulled the bottle towards himself and started emptying it in his glass.

"Bas kar saale, fifteen minutes back you were shouting at the fourth one."

"That's the charisma of daaru, just like love; the more you have it, for more it impels", he gulped, burped and laid down on the floor, "tu mera bhai hai", came his faded voice after a while and he closed his eyes.

Knowing it to be the breaking point line, Aarav said nothing but picked up his glass and raised it to his mouth to gulp it. His gaze fell on the computer screen.

"Oye the system's up", he kicked Neil.

"Hmmm", was all he replied.

"Asshole", Aarav breathed to himself. He stood up with a cigarette in between his lips, walked up to the system and logged in to Facebook.

The message icon on the top left side said 1, he clicked on it.

"Hii smarty", it said. He read the name, Metro Gal, no profile picture. 'Do I know you Ms Metro?' he thought, typed the same and clicked on send. He started scrolling down the page to go through the posts. He loved reading them. One of them said, "Love isn't complicated, people are", he smiled. Just then, the message icon turned red with the number 1 flashed on it, he clicked.

"No u don't... but wud u like to?" It was metro gal again. Aarav frowned and smiled, 'This is interesting', he thought, and typed, "so u're online, upld ur pic and thn I'll dcide, an btw who told u I'm smart?" and clicked on send.

Metro gal: U trespasd the ladies coach tht day... I was there… and u've got a clear face view pic uplded on ur accnt!! wat tuk u so long to reply???

Aarav Khanna: ya 14th Feb... I rmmbr…how come u found me on Fb???...I'm replying instantly, is it reaching late??

Metro gal: u shoutd out ur name loudly ovr the phn… I srchd and found u☺ …I'm not talkin abt nw…chek d date of the frst msg!!!

Offline messages turned into a chat. Aarav checked the date of first message, it was 14 Feb 2012, 9.47 a.m.

Aarav Khanna: wow u're smart and as far as I rmmbr... 9.47 a.m, I ws in the metro, so u opnd a fake acnt on Fb and txd me thn only?? Don't login tht oftn…tht's y!!! and whch one were u…upld ur pic.

Metro gal: Ya I opnd the acnt thn only... Jst wantd to make my Valentines Day and birthday a lil interstng… bt u ddn't rply☹!!

Aarav Khanna: wow...Valentines Day is ur birthday!! Happy belatd birthday ☺!!

Metro gal: thnk u☺

Aarav Khanna: nw madam wud u pls tel me which one were u?? And u stay logd in to ths fake accnt, ol the time?"

Metro gal: the one in the mini skirt☺!! No jst logd in to chk u replied or nt☺

Aarav Khanna: I don't rmmbr any minni minni!!

Metro gal: Wat?? U kept lookin at my legs, ol d way☺... an nw u don't even rmmbr???

Aarav Khanna: shut up... I'm no Gajni... I don't forget things... not atlst a mini skrt!!

Metro gal: hehe... I ws the one in the blck shades at the door... I even pasd a smile jst before debordin... u wr ogling!!

Aarav stood up from the chair, "God!! Can't believe this", he kicked Neil, "abe uth, look this is a miracle." Neil made no reflexes, Aarav bent down to pick up the last bottle of beer, kicked him again and recommenced the position to continue with that racy turn.

Metro gal: hey u thr??

Aarav Khanna: ya ya... ws jst takin my medicine!! There ws a fair gal wid pimples, she ws staring madly tht day, thot this is she!!

Metro gal: What medicine?? thot?? Or u wantd ths to be her!!☺

Aarav looked at the bottle and smiled.

Aarav Khanna: nothng jst one fr the cold!! ya... bt that's ok!! U're also gud... kaam chal jayega☺!!

Metro gal: hehe... chala le yaar kaam... at times u have to compromise... that's lyf☺

Aarav Khanna: hahaha... u're not a typical kind.

Metro gal: wat do u mean??

Aarav Khanna: nthng... lt it b!!

Metro gal: so u got the job??

Aarav Khanna: God!! Are u a detective or somthng... hw come u knw I ws goin fr an interview that day???

Metro gal: hehe... I heard u talkin to that fat guy!! So u got it??

Aarav Khanna: Ok!! Ya I got it!! And hey wats ur name btw... the real one!!

Metro gal: grt... party thn!! Ada!!

Aarav Khanna: Wow that's a beautiful name.

Metro gal: Thank you☺...ur name is nice as wel...infct thts one of the resons I txd u!!

Aarav Khanna: really??...thnks!! wat r the other ones pls☺??

Metro gal: umm ur eyes...ur hair...ur drsng sense...tht blck shrt ws realy brth takin☺

Aarav Khanna: Love at first sight...ha??

Metro gal: Hey don't get ideas...no luv shuv...k!!

Aarav Khanna: so, you just drooled over my luks???

Metro gal: yup!!... and I still am☺

Aarav Khanna: haha u're so candid!! Thts y I sd u're nt typical!! So, u keep txtng every other smart guy??

Metro gal: I wish!! But not ol of thm yell their names in public, with whch thy have an fb accnt☺

Aarav Khanna: hehe...poor u!! u knw wat... that day I ws almst abt to follow u...bt before I cud choose betwn u and the job...the damn doors got closd☹

Metro gal: Really?? Bt u sd u wr intrstd in Ms. Acne☺

Aarav Khanna: Thr is no Ms. Acne!! The momnt I heard u...I ws lookin at u!!

Metro gal: when did u hear me??

Aarav Khanna: u wr talkin ovr the phn.

Metro gal: but I ws talkin so slowly.

Aarav Khanna: and I ws listenin so keenly.

Metro gal: hehe...so u liked my voice??

Aarav Khanna: It ws msmrzin!!

Metro gal: thnk u thnk u!! hey u're nt at a café? R u?

Arav Khanna: why?

Metro gal: if u've got internet cnctn…y didn't u rply earlier??

Aarav Khanna: I'm at a frnd's place…I don hav internt…neithr in my phn nor in my computr!!

Metro gal: why?? U don lyk surfing??

Aarav Khanna: no I don't!! seems lyk u do!!

Metro gal: ya a lot!! Thers a lot…Fb…yahoo…google…you tube or may be a porn site sometimes☺!

Aarav Khanna: hehe …u're alwys ths open??

Metro gal: no…bt thr r ppl u cn be urslf with!!

Aarav Khanna: why do u thnk I'm one of those??

Metro gal: don knw!! Bt thrs smthng abt u whch touchd me mysteriously…can't put it in wrds!! And I'm chatin wid u fr d last 20 mins…bt thrs no stranger kind'o feelin..!!

Aarav kept looking at the answer for a few seconds, and smiled at her fair acknowledgement, happening to sound exactly like his own feelings, since the day he saw her for the first time.

Metro gal: U thr??

Aarav Khanna: Yup!! So wat do u do metro gal…aprt frm watchin porn☺?

Metro gal: I dream!!!

Aarav Khanna: Thank god u've atlst one typical girlish wont!! Bt I'm talkin abt ur profsn??

Metro gal: hehe…I'm a 3rd year student of a borng engnrng colg☹…an whr do u wrk??

Aarav Khanna: great!! Wat branch?? whch colg?? I wrk wd a call centre!!

Metro gal: wow mst be fun!! Mechanical!! St. Jacob Engineering College!!

Aarav Khanna: wats so pleasant abt makin calls?? Wat made u choose mechanical??

Metro gal: hv hrd thngs abt cal cntrs☺!! I wantd to do aerospace eng and go to NASA...bt cudn't☹...thts y mechncl...hazy bt hopes are stl alive...mechancl fits evrwhr u knw☺!! U alwys wantd to b a cal cntr exctv??

Aarav Khanna: what thngs?? I nevr wantd to b anything...thts y I'm nthng...wrkin to make the ends meet...thts it!!

Metro gal: ummm that u guys hv lots an lots of partys... nght clubs... discos.

Aarav Khanna: not ol of us... I don do tht!!

Metro gal: y u don lyk partys??

Aarav Khanna: no...jst through wid it...hd enough!!

Metro gal: I've nvr been to a nght club...ppl here r soooo boring...studies ol the tym☹ wl u take me to one...smday??

Aarav Khanna: sure!!

Metro gal: hey u've a gf?

Aarav curled his fingers, close to the keyboard, back in his palm and gave the question a little thought. "No", he typed a few seconds later.

Metro gal: u're lying

Aarav Khanna: y do u thnk so??

Metro gal: u tuk a few extra secnds to rply...u're hiding smthng☺

Aarav Khanna: God!! Frgt NASA...join CIA...u'll have a grt career thr.

Metro gal: hehe...so I ws rit??

Aarav Khanna: ya thr is a gal ...wt bout u??

Metro gal: no bf☹...had one back in Goa, wen I ws in school!!

Aarav Khanna: wow u're frm Goa??

Metro gal: y u delhites trt outstatn ppl lyk aliens...I'm frm Goa nt saturn.

Aarav Khanna: hehe…tuchy topic, I gues!! An I'm nt a delhite…I'm frm Jaipur

Metro gal: wow Jaipur!! Pink city!!

Aarav Khanna: nw rn't u treatin me lyk an alien☺

Metro gal: hehe…so ur gf wrks wid u?... u two r in live in??

Aarav Khanna: u assume too much… I stay alone… she wrks wid designer Jaspreet kaur, 'The J's' owner!!

Metro gal: Is ur gf a fashion designr?

Aarav Khanna: yup

Metro gal: great!! Is tht y u're so wel drsd☺?? Hw did u two meet?

Aarav Khanna: haha…at the clg

Metro gal: k…so u too r a fashn desgnr…usng u're fashn sense to attract sexy gals at call centr…ha☺

Aarav Khanna: strange!

Metro gal: wat??

Aarav Khanna: y didn't u ask …wat I'm doin in the call cntr wrld…being a fashion designer??

Metro gal: It's ur lyf…u mst b comfrtbl wrkin thr…y shud I ask tht!!

Aarav smiled at her answer, 'she is really different, Should I ask her out', as he was thinking, her message flashed, "U thr??"

Aarav Khanna: u're so impatient

Metro gal: hehe…thts d way I am!!

Aarav Khanna: Wat r u doin tomrw?? Wud u like to hv a cup of coffee wid me??

He waited for few seconds, there was no reply.

Aarav Khanna: u thr??

Still no reply.

Aarav Khanna: thinkin abt the proposal?? Luk u don't hv to b confusd…u cn say no…I won't mind

He kept looking at the screen for about a minute or two, but there was no response. 'Girls, at the end of the day, will be girls.' He felt offended. 'I shouldn't have asked this.' He gulped the left-over beer in a single breath… turned off the computer and went to bed.

***

"Aarav, Aarav", Neil said, rubbing his shoulder gently. He opened his eyes and took a few seconds to put himself together.

"What?" He muttered slowly, pressing against his temple.

"It's one O'clock man, lunch's ready, get up."

"Really?" Aarav was still holding his head.

"That's because we didn't have dinner last night, nimbu pani?" Neil pointed at his headache.

"No", Aarav said with one eye closed. He opened the eye and looked at Neil, "cigarette's left?" he said sluggishly.

"I've cooked rice and some potato, gonna go downstairs to get a packet of pickle", Neil said throwing the cigarette and match box towards him as he hurried out. Aarav took one out and as he was about to light it, Neil showed up again, with half his body inside the flat, holding the door with one hand and the side wall with another, "Yamaha is auditioning bands for their official launch party, one of my band members just called, wanna come along?" he said loudly. Aarav opened both his eyes wide, thought for a few seconds and answered, "go get the pickle first". "Okay", Neil replied and pulled the door.

Aarav lit the cigarette, took a puff and while he was letting the smoke out, his gaze fell on the computer at the other end of the room. He kept looking at it for a while, "was it a dream?" He smiled as he got down from the bed and started walking towards the bathroom. Something stopped him midway, he walked back up to the system, turned it on and headed for a shower.

***

"You turned it on?" On seeing Aarav coming out of the bathroom, Neil asked, pointing towards the computer.

"You are back, ya I did it, is it up?"

"Not yet."

"Where did you get this garbage from? 20 minutes and it's still not synchronized. You got the pickle?"

"Yup", Neil raised the pickle packet to show him.

"Got a t-shirt? This stinks", Aarav said, smelling his shirt. Neil walked towards the wardrobe. "A washed one", Aarav added loudly.

"Choose", Neil showed him three t-shirts.

"Any one will do yaar, gonna be wearing it under the jacket anyway."

"You change jackets almost everyday man, how many of them have you got, by the way? Behanchoo all branded", Neil sounded surprised. Aarav smiled innocently.

"So you're coming with us?" Neil changed the topic while keeping the t-shirts back in the wardrobe, after throwing one on the bed.

"Alright, but how long is that gonna take?" Aarav inquired while drying his hair with a hand towel.

"Four hours, may be five".

"Five hours!!" Aarav exclaimed with a low voice, raising his brows.

"The system's up." Neil didn't seem to hear his suppressed exclamation.

"What?"

"The sytem is up", Neil repeated, in a higher pitch this time.

"Really", towel clad Aarav almost ran towards it and logged in to Fb. Second icon from the left had number 3 flashing over it. He clicked on it.

Metro gal: u thr??

Metro gal: sry, actualy lost the conctvty☹

Metro gal: hey thts a gud idea...hw bout tmrw aftrnun...my cell number is 99xxxxxxxx, call me and lt me knw the time and place u wnt me to come.

He read all the messages that showed as received around 5 in the morning in a breath. "Thank god!!" he released the breath, looking at the messages and the timing again, 'so you stayed up all night to text me?' he thought and smiled. "Where's my cell phone?" he turned his head to look for it. Neil tilted his head towards the bed, "there". Aarav walked upto the bed and picked up his cell. Two missed calls and a message from Shayna; the phone was on silent mode. The message said, "had your dinner? Call me once u're free", he gritted his teeth and closed his eyes, "shit"he uttered slowly..

"Is everything okay?" Neil's voice brought him back.

"Ya" he shrugged and walked back to the computer and copied the number to his cell phone. When he turned, Neil was standing right behind him.

"Jesus!! You scared me man", Aarav cried out.

Neil frowned, "Whats going on?"

"Nothing"

"Really?" Neil widened his eyes. This time he was looking at the computer screen, "who's this metro gal?"

"C'mon, let's have your rice and potato, I'll tell you", he pushed Neil, while typing a message on his cell, "so hw bout selct city mall at 3 o' clock -Aarav", he wrote and sent it to Ada.

"When I was going to Midllan for the interview on 14th, I saw this girl in the metro, she saw me too", Aarav looked at his cell phone twice during this sentence, expecting her quick reply.

"Then?" Neil said while offering some more rice.

"No, no", Aarav pulled his bowl back.

"So, you two became friends that day?"

"No, I called up the HR as I was getting late and I said my name loudly over the phone, she searched me on facebook and messaged me at the same moment, but I saw it only yesterday."

"Wow, strangest case ever", with both ends of the lips bent downwards, Neil frowned. Aarav shrugged with a thin smile on his face. "Ghnnnnn…ghnnnn", his cell vibrated. It was Ada.

"Wht do I need to tell the auto drvr...slct city mall? cmin frm kalkaji...wl I rch thr in an hour... it's 2 rit nw??" was the message.

"Just add Malviya Nagar to it to avoid any confusion...ya u'll rch...cal me as soon as u r thr", he replied.

"Where do I need to keep this?" Aarav stood up with the empty bowl. Neil pointed towards the kitchen as his mouth was full of rice. Aarav went inside the kitchen. "Don't wash it, I'll do that later", with a lot of rice in his mouth, Neil managed to speak, after swallowing some of it. Aarav came back, put his jeans on and as he was looking at the t-shirt, her message flashed in his mind, *tht blck shrt ws realy breath takin*. He thought for a while and turned towards Neil, "you've got a black shirt?"

"Ya got one", Neil switched his eyesight from Aarav to the wardrobe, "but you asked for a t-shirt", he added. "Changed my mind." Aarav walked towards the relevant end.

"Let me also wear a shirt, then we'll look like brothers", done with his lunch, Neil stood up.

"Aaaa... Neil I'm not coming with you", Aarav said slowly, biting his lower lip.

"But you said you are."

"Gotta meet someone", after putting the shirt on, Aarav was sitting on the chair, slipping his feet into his shoes.

"Who?" Neil was surprised. Aarav looked towards him, "Ada, the metro girl", he winked.

"Behanchoo"

***

A little ahead of the main entrance of the mall, Aarav stood leaning against a five foot pillar-like structure in front of the three foot boundary wall, with a lighted cigarette in his left hand and his cell phone in the right one. He looked at the time. It was 3.10 p.m. 'Shall I call her?' he thought, looking at the cell phone's display. "Naah!!" he made a typical sound pressing his tongue against the palate, shook his head, in rejection of his own statement. "Call her first and you lose the credit", he justified himself while taking the last puff of his cigarette and kept the cell back in his pocket.

Every passing auto was making him astir. 'Quite a few affairs and many a dates, but none agented this longing', he thought to himself as he took his cell out again, completely aware of the time, looked at the display and kept it back. He wasn't much into this habit of slipping the cell phone in and out of the pocket, but clearly the anxiety was compelling him to do so. He put his little finger in between his teeth and started chewing the not-so long nail - another way to curb that anxiety. But figuring out its inefficiency, he started walking towards the tea stall on the footpath ahead, to buy himself another cigarette, thinking that'll work. "Ghnnn... ghnnn", midway, he felt the vibration of his phone and pulled it out in a fraction of second, it was 'Ada'. He sighed in relief.

"Hiii, have y ou reached?" he said calmly, receiving the call after around ten seconds. Just didn't want her to know that he was waiting for her call with his cell in his hand. "Ya I'm in front of this blue building, with fountains in its lawn, where are you?"

'Wow what a voice', he wanted to say. "That's Select City Mall. Stay put, just about to reach, I'm on my way", he didn't want to defy his own experiences with girls. One of his mantras was 'you make them wait and they'll value you.' He was certainly quite decisive with its use.

"Alright", she said cutely and hung up.

"She is not acting typical, then why am I?" he laughed faintly. "One Marlboro light and an orbit", he had already reached the tea stall. 'I've to walk to the other end of the mall', he explained his purchase to himself; usual practice among smokers, finding a reason every time.

***

'Maroon midi with a matching fluffy jacket, well complemented by a leather handbag' There was only one girl in front of the fountain. He saw her from a distance. She was looking into the artificial pond in the lawn, hair fallen carelessly, covering almost all of her face. He went close to her, "found the pearl?" he asked at once.

"Oh!" she looked at him with a smile, removing the hair from her face with her fingers, "Hii", she added after a while and forwarded her hand. Those open dense black hair, falling to and forth on her fair cute face, making those big black eyes blink like twinkling stars, made him sigh involuntarily. But he tried his best not to let it get noticed.

"So, any trouble reaching here?" Aarav asked after a firm handshake. She shook her head with the same cute smile. "This is for you", she handed him a Dairy milk chocolate a second later. *No flowers, no chocolates, you shameless - is that what she means?* He thought while taking it. "Thank you", he said slowly. What else could he say?

Silent as they were, they started walking towards the MGF mall. On a date like this, silence is a usual start and walking anywhere, just like that, is a usual movement.

After a 10 minute walk, Aarav broke the silence, "you're lookin taller in this midi". You need at least something, even if something stupid, to kick start a conversation.

She just showed him her heels and of course, wouldn't stop smiling.

"Oh! So that's the secret", he said, "actually in fitting dresses like this you tend to look a little taller", he flaunted his fashion knowledge.

"You're looking good," she said, perhaps wanting him to say that. She shot for it the other way.

"So are you." It worked!

"Didn't get enough time, you texted at two asking to come at three, got dressed in just 15 minutes", she was looking at her dress.

"Actually, I woke up late today", gauging her complaint, he justified the delay.

Silence again! 'On the first date, you gotta keep saying something or else they will use terms like, "boring tha", at your back', Aarav's experiences couldn't cease to roar inside him.

"So, is your girl friend working today?" Before he could say anything else, she took the initiative.

"Why?" He laughed. "Why aren't you with her then?" she asked again.

"Oh! Met her yesterday only."

"Why not today again?" she shrugged.

"She had to go out with her friends", he lied.

"What if she happens to be around and sees you with me."

"So what?"

"She might get the wrong idea."

"Or the right one", he winked. A habitual flirt just can't resist a chance.

"Forget it", she said, giggling.

"Really? Why are you here then?" Her titter instigated his enquiry.

She shrugged ignoring his question, tilted her head on one side with a smile that swept him off his feet. He kept looking into her beautiful eyes for a while, "Seems like I have seen these eyes before", he said on a serious note, still looking into them.

"Shahrukh to Kajol, DDLJ", she said in the same cadence.

He burst into laughter after taking a couple of seconds to understand it, "coffee?" He was still laughing.

"Sure." By now they had reached the MGF mall. Aarav looked around, "there it is!" he said looking at the Barista.

"Is there a Pizza Hut?" she enquired.

"May be, not sure", he jerked his shoulders. "You wanna have pizza?"

"No, just wanted to get you something special", she replied with a smile.

"And what is it?" he sounded surprised. She said nothing but smiled again. 'What could possibly be so special at Pizza Hut?' he thought.

After a refreshing Mocha and sandwiches at Barista, they were strolling inside the mall. "So, how's your studies going?" Aarav asked.

"Good".

"So, you stay alone?"

"No, hostel", she said, "but once I'm in the final year this August, I'll rent a flat", she seemed happy at her decision.

"Alone?" pat he questioned. Boys do like to enquire these things.

"No, with a friend."

"Boy friend, ha", he smiled wickedly.

"Told ya, I don't have one."

"Why? Isn't there a smart guy in your college?"

"Ummm…there are. But those who are handsome are book worms and boring, those who are not boring are weird and those who are neither boring nor weird are unfortunately not that good looking".

"Wow, what an answer", he laughed, "there must be one at least".

"Not that I know of."

"But there must be a lot of guys after you."

"Why?"

"Ummm… you are beautiful, intelligent and I have heard there's extreme scarcity of girls at engineering colleges, so you must be topping the charts of most desirable girls", he smiled.

She smiled, "none touched my heart yet, I'm still waiting for my dream boy".

"So just casual dates, that's it."

"No, it's my first date".

"Really?" he didn't believe it. 'So, charming, so independent and first date?' he thought.

"Why a date with me then?" he asked.

"Don't know, like I said yesterday, there is something about you which attracted me, something different", she was looking at him with a blank expression, but she sounded honest, "but it's not love, okay", she said smilingly, bringing herself back to the moment.

They remained silent for a while. It was their third round across the corridor of the ground floor.

"Hey what's that?" looking at the statues with thick gown and hood, she shouted in excitement.

"There's an icebar upstairs", he said

"Bar, wow, haven't boozed in years."

"Wanna go for it then?"

"No!" Her refusal seemed more like a yes.

"C'mon", he dragged her.

***

"And santa fell on the ground", Aarav completed some stupid santa banta joke.

She laughed uncontrollably with both her hands on her flat belly. That's the bad part of alcohol, it makes you crack nonsense jokes. But the good part is that it makes you laugh at them.

Not too drunk, but enough to stand out of the normally behaving class, they kept laughing, sitting on a bench in the premises of the mall. Multiple jets of water projected artificially from the ground and the retrenching sunlight through the scattered clouds, seemed so refreshing. Or may be it's just the company that makes things pleasant and beautiful.

"So you like Delhi? It's pretty different from Goa, ha?" Aarav put both his hands behind his head and stretched his legs to make himself comfortable.

"Ya Delhi is good but I certainly miss Goa", she said.

"The beaches and bonfires?"

"That's for tourists, we don't go to beaches every evening and light bonfires."

"Really?"

"Yaa... would you go to the forts in Jaipur everyday, when you were there?"

"Alright, but when you take me to Goa, show me the beaches with bikini clad girls running all around like bay watch", he forced a long breath out. She smiled. "And we'll go for a beach walk on a full moon night", he added. She kept smiling. "You'll take me along, won't you?" a little confused with her smile, he asked.

"What if I won't?" she replied.

"Then I'll come after you, someday". He looked straight into her eyes. They remained silent. Some imaginations are enough to stir those unknown sentiments.

"So how long have you been in Delhi?" Ada preferred to break the silence.

"Umm... six years"

"You like it?"

"Not much", he replied after a while, with bent lips and raised shoulders.

"Why are you here then?"

"Because of them", he said very seriously, signaling towards a romping group of college girls.

She burst into laughter, "you really like girls, don't you?"

"Sexy Delhi girls", he smiled and jerked his right brow.

"Is that why you entered the ladies coach that day?" she widened her eyes.

"No, that was by accident", he mocked a frightened face.

"You remember when that aunty in the metro asked you to leave, your expressions were quite a vision", she laughed.

"Yaa... you can argue with a bouncer of a disco in Gurgaon but not with an aunty from Delhi," he nodded being dramatically pensive, adding another scale to her laughter.

"No really, I'm serious" He really was. "You know one day...", he turned towards her to prove his point, "... wow!!", he said slowly, on seeing a girl in a snug fit jeans, walking past them, right behind Ada. He forgot his point and got his eyesight glued on her curves. Ada turned her head back, to see what made him go numb suddenly. She then looked back at Aarav, whose head was rotating slowly, following that girl, as if tied to her back by some invisible cosmic rope. Ada winked, "she is good... ha?"

"Good?" he turned towards her, "she can actually beat Jlo with those", he sighed.

"You wanna get her?"

"Aaah... I wish", he hit his chest.

"C'mon lets follow her", she stood up and commanded like an army officer, with one hand straight downward and the other pointing at the target.

"You shouldn't have had three pegs, two is your limit I guess ", he said, astounded by her antic.

"Come na!!" she ignored his comment and pulled him by his hand. He let her have her way, reluctantly willing to participate in that idiotic act and they started walking behind the girl, laughing intermittently. Hearing their laughter the girl stopped and turned around for a moment and they suddenly took a right turn. After a few seconds, they took the previous direction again.

"She is gone!!" Ada said loudly. They couldn't see her. "Perhaps she took a left turn over there", he replied. "Cover me", Ada took the lead. "Alright." They were behaving like some secret agents from Hollywood movies.

"Are you two following me?" The girl was standing in front of Archie's gallery, right after the turn. They both froze, as if the girl had said 'statue'.

"Ya... he likes you", Ada pointed towards Aarav, a couple seconds later.

"What!!" the girl exclaimed.

"No no, sorry, she is just drunk", Aarav pulled her by her elbow.

"God, are you crazy?" Aarav said slowly, although they had walked much ahead of the girl now. Ada kept laughing with her hand on her mouth. Their walking pace was much faster and they maintained it, till they reached the pavement on the other side of the mall, close to the main road.

"Never do it again, you'll go to hostel and I'll land up in jail", Aarav was smiling at her stupidity.

"Oh! Hostel! God I completely forgot that, what's the time?"

"Why, what happened?" he asked while taking out the cell.

"Gotta head back."

"So early?" he appeared surprised.

"Ya hostel gate closes by eight", she sounded a little sad.

The cloudy sky was turning darker with only a few streaks of light at the horizon. Except for some chirping birds, it was just the two of them, at that secluded end. The breeze felt colder, but there was a warmth of those veiled feelings, deep inside.

"It's Sunday evening, lesser traffic, you can take an auto after ten or fifteen minutes", he didn't want her to leave.

"Okay", she agreed. She didn't want to leave either.

As if on cue, it started raining - perhaps the weather wanted the same.

"Oh God! Rain in February?" Ada shouted. "DTC buses and rain in Delhi, always unexpected", Aarav held her hand and they both ran to take shelter. They housed themselves under a dense tree along the road. "I must go now", she said slowly and slipped her hand from his. Aarav looked at her face, the water droplets pretended to be shining gems embedded on a fine piece of white marble and a few strands of wet hair fell across like some graceful ancient art on it. It took him a while to understand what she said. "Oh, yes", he switched his gaze, wiping his face and waved at a passing auto. It didn't stop. "These auto drivers I tell you", he turned towards her. She smiled softly with a hint of shyness. He kept looking at her, the strands still intact, bothering him for some unknown reason. He raised his hand slowly towards her face, her smile ceased with the movement. His dark brown eyes laid firm on her black ones, hearts pounding like door knocks. He touched her face with his finger, she half closed her eyes. "Where do you wanna go?" a rustic tone, came hurling from behind. It was the same auto driver. It probably took him a while to apply brakes after the wave and he had driven back.

"Aaa... kalkaji", it took Aarav a couple of seconds to pull himself together.

"Hundred rupees", the driver said.

She got inside the auto. "Bye", he said softly and forwarded his hand. She held it and smiled sadly but didn't say anything. Maybe she wanted to, but the stupid driver moved the vehicle. Their hands parted.

Only a second later Aarav ran after the auto, "hey whats your complete name?"

"Ada Maciel", she smiled and waved bye.

***

"Wow Shay that's great, three months official tour to Mumbai ha! That sounds really good", standing in his balcony at 11 in the night, talking over the phone, with a bottle of beer in hand, Aarav seemed really happy for her. "So when are you leaving?"

"Day after tomorrow, wish you were coming along", she said sadly.

"I'm always along, distances can't sever friends," he consoled her.

"I don't understand why you always refer to me as a friend, just a friend".

He remained silent. "You don't love me", her voice sunk. He still couldn't answer, he didn't have one. He was well aware of his feelings, he just did not have the guts to admit them to her. Mainly because he did not want to hurt her. "Aaru you're there?" he heard her, drawing deep breaths.

"Ya, I'm here, how was your day?" he changed the topic, like always.

"Just the usual month end, Sunday meeting which went extra long, discussing this Mumbai event. How was yours?" she replied slowly after a while.

"Umm... it was good, accompanied Neil and his band for an audition", Ada's smiling face flashed in his mind, as he lied.

"Must have been fun ha?"

"Yaa... so packing all done?"

"Almost, you had your dinner?"

"Almost", he looked at the remaining amount of beer in his bottle and burped slightly.

"What time are you leaving for work tomorrow?" she asked.

"Around four in the evening, why?"

"Just wanted to see you and hug you once before leaving for Mumbai. Day after tomorrow it's gonna be real hectic", she went a little slow with her request, fearing denial. 'God! Why are girls so dramatic all the time?' he thought, "So you want me to be there?"

"No, don't wanna bother you, I'll come down to your place if I manage to get off work early tomorrow"

"Alright", he said sluggishly.

"You sound tired, go get some good sleep."

"Hmm..."

"Bye jaan, good night, love you", she said joyfully.

"Love you too", he copied her tone, while walking back into his room.

"Liar", she giggled.

"Bye", he said slowly and disconnected the call, gulped the left over beer in a single sip and kept the bottle on the floor, beside the sofa. He walked upto his bed, fell on it and closed his eyes.

'Ada Maciel, the way you said your name, wow'. He couldn't stop thinking about her. Those intense black eyes, kept hovering in his mind for long. 'It's not that I haven't seen a girl as beautiful, but there's something special about you, something really different', he thought and only after a second, realized that she also had said the same thing. He smiled, 'is it love?' he kept smiling for a while, but it soon disappeared, 'are you crazy?' he denounced himself a little later, tossed on the bed and tried to sleep.

'Shall I text her?' he opened his eyes after a few minutes, finding it real hard to sleep. Thinking for a moment, he pulled his cell lying on the other end of the bed with his leg, took it in his hand when it came within his reach and wondered what to write. Suddenly a message flashed on the screen, it was Ada. He was surprised and happy, 'what timing ha?' He thought and opened the message. "Thnks fr a wnderful evening", it said. He kept smiling for a while and then typed, "so it tuk u five hrs to decide tht?" and sent it to her.

"Hehe…no ws bz wid a projct…hv to submt it tmrw! Y r u awake at ths time? Or did I wake u up?" She replied within seconds.

Aarav: u didn't wake me up…u jst won't let me sleep!!

Ada: wht? :-)

Aarav: ya I ws tryin to… but cudn't stop thinkin abt u!!

Ada: me? realy? wat?

Aarav: ya I ws wndering wat did u want to buy me frm pizza hut!!

Ada: hehe…it's a surprise!! Nxt time fr sure…k!! Nw tell me y r u still awake?

Aarav: yaar we r cal cntr ppl…we sleep ol day like asses and stay awake ol nit like owls!!:-(

Ada: hahaha…

Aarav: so u stay awake ths late every day?

Ada: ya mostly!! V study till 11 and thn its gossip time☺

Aarav: Ok!!So it's time fr ur daily dose of gossip…stp chatng an go fr it…else u might fall sick tmrw☺

Ada: hehe…no already had it…full fr the day!!

Aarav: thnk god!! So spoke to ur frnds abt ur frst date?

Ada: ya…showd them ur pic as wel… on fb☺

Aarav: realy? So wat ws thr reaction☺

Ada: sm jealos…sm happy fr me!!

Aarav: happy fr u…ha!! wat is tht supsd to mean??:-)

Ada: thy thnk I'm in luv!!

Aarav: an wat do u thnk??

Ada: thy r wrng☺

Aarav: realy??☹

Ada: y?? u wnt me to fall fr u???

Aarav: I thot… u alrdy hav☺

Ada: keep gtng ideas☺!! U spoke to ur gf??

Aarav: abt wat…brk up…sry havn't…bt w'll do tht soon…once u say yes?

Ada: hehe…u flrt like ths wid ol d grls…don't u?

Aarav: wat if I'm serious ths time???

Ada: oh please!!

Aarav: no bt srsly…I hv startd flng smthng fr u!!!

Ada: ya same here…bt tht smthng is nt luv!!!

Aarav: so wat acrdng to u is luv!!

Ada: luv defines evrythng… but it can't itself be defined. It's a divine feeling, beyond definition, perhaps even beyond life and death!!

Aarav: wow!!

Ada: ok tel me hw deep is ur relatn wid ur gf… and wats hr name btw!!

Aarav: don knw yaar… I mean we are frnds since clg… she says she luvs me… an I do hv a soft corner fr her… thts it! Shayna.

Ada: may b u guys need sm time!! Hey thts a nice name!!

Aarav: Time?? it's already bn like 6 yrs nw!! U evr luvd smone lyk ths…I mean… beyond life an death kindzz??

Ada: nopes!!

Aarav: wat bout ur ex-bf??

Ada: hehe I lied…actly tht ws one sided crush…nt a luv affair!! I ws in class 6th and had a big crush on a cute guy…one day his father was tarnsfrd somewhr in Gujrat…an thy ol movd.

Aarav: O!! cho chad☹

Ada: ya I even cried once…:-)

Aarav: an' y do u thnk it ws jst a crush…an nt luv???

Ada: becuz I flt tht fr many a guys…mostly good lukin!! :-)

Aarav: haha!! Grls usually don't acpt these thngs!!

Ada: wats wrng wid acptng the truth…

Aarav: ok…so no serious relatnshp so far…any hanky panky kindzzz thn☺???

Ada: hanky panky???

Aarav: ya…jst kisng…tchng…u knw!!:-)

Ada: hehe…no…bcuz fr me…tht holds no meaning widout luv!!

Aarav: true!!

Ada: can I ask u smthng???

Aarav: sure!

Ada: if u don't luv shayna…y r u wid hr thn??

Aarav: yar she knws tht I don luv hr…bt still she is wid me…don knw y!! an' I treat hr as a gud frnd…so don' wanna hurt hr

Ada: thnk god!!

Aarav: wat??

Ada: the rsn is not hanky panky!!

Aarav: hahaha…

Ada: so not shayna…nybody else u hv evr bn in luv wid??

Aarav: falln fr many a girls…but tht divine kindzz…not yet!!

Ada: so jst casual flirting so far…ha??

Aarav: ya u cn say tht…during clg I ws a celebratd flirt!!

Ada: u're still quite gud☺…btw whch clg u did ur fashn desgnin frm??

Aarav: thnk u thnk u!! NIFT!!

Ada: wow!! Thts cool…frm Delhi brnch??

Aarav: ya…

Ada: whr in Delhi is it?

Aarav: Hauz Khas

Ada: whr is Hauz Khas??

Aarav: it's near IIT Delhi!! Seems lyk u don knw mch abt Delhi!!

Ada: ya☹…we've only been to CP a few times… havn't evn seen jama masjid and lal kila☹

Aarav: lal kila??? It's a borin fort…

Ada: bt I do wanna go thr…wl u take me??

Aarav: so u need a guide!!

Ada: hehe…plss na!! I'll gv u dairy milk!!

He burst into laughter on reading her message.

Aarav: wat?? U thnk u cn lure me wid a mere dairy milk…frgt it☺!!

Ada: alrit two dairy milks…deal??

Aarav: hehe…deal!!

Ada: grt!! Nxt Tuesday thrs a test in the clg☹…hw bout nxt to nxt Sunday??

Aarav: ths is my last week of trainin…so week offs wl be sat and sun!! nt sure abt nxt sun!!

Ada: oou☹!! So Sunday is nt alwys a holiday fr u??

Aarav: nopes!!

Ada: ok…lets meet ths Sunday thn…if it's ok wid u!!

Aarav: okie dokie!!

Ada: ☺☺

Aarav: sooo happy ha…finaly u got ur guide aftr three yrs…at four ths fine morning!!

Ada: God!! We hav bn chatng for four hrs!!...didn't realize!!

Aarav: wat time u hv to go to the clg??

Ada: clses starts at 9…thn the projct thng…thn practicals till 4!! It's a long day☹

Aarav: gt some sleep thn!!

Ada: ya…gd nit…sweet drmzz☺!!

Aarav: sweet??...wish me sexy ones!! Gd nit…an gud luck fr tht projct☺!!

Ada: hehe…gd nit…sexy drmzz!! Thnks☺

***

The irritating sound of his phone's alarm woke him up. That acoustic torture was his own conscious choice, for his otherwise deep sleep. "It's 2.30", he said to himself eyes still closed, and a hand crawling on bed in the direction of the abiding tease. He turned the alarm off and lay glued to the bed for a while, phone still in his hand. 'I'll give you dairymilk', her message flashed in his mind turning into an imagination of her, saying that to him with her head tilted on one side. A big smile floated across his face. An unknown urge made him bring the phone close to read a couple of messages from the last conversation and to his surprise he found an unread one from Ada at 8.50 a.m, 'gud mrnin mr. guide☺☺'. His smile stretched to its limit. Smileys from a person you were already smiling for, are likely to cause it. He sent "gud mrnin☺!" in return, got down from the bed and went for a shower.

***

He looked annoyed holding the turned on tap of the sink in his kitchen, with no signs of water in it. He hit it twice with his palm and after a few seconds, water rushed out with huge pressure, drenching him thoroughly. "Thank god!! Today it took just a minute", he sighed, wiping the water from his hands and face and started washing a pan for making Maggi, the official life savior of Indian bachelors.

"Take a left turn just after the metro station and you will see Reliance Fresh around two hundred metres ahead. Call me once you reach there", Aarav was guiding the cab driver for his pickup point, "and the pick time is four so don't come before that". He only got a click in return. He looked at the time, it was 3.22 p.m. 'Shayna said yesterday, she is gonna come'. He seemed thoughtful sitting on the sofa with a coffee tumbler and noodles pan on the table in front. He dialed her number, "hey Aaaru", she chirped, receiving the call after around six rings.

"Hii", Aarav resonated her tone.

"You know what, Jaspreet has given a half day off to all the employees who are selected for these Mumbai events, and PVR and KFC vouchers to enjoy it!!"

"Great, the bitch is showing some improvement now".

"She is not that bad yaar".

"Anyway, I thought you were coming down to my place".

"Oh! Aaru, were you waiting for me, so sorry shona, you know na how my colleagues are, they insisted so I had to …"

"That's okay, I'm not asking for any explanation".

"Sorry jaan".

"That's okay Shay, chill, call me tomorrow, I'll try to meet you, bye".

"Bye, love you".

'She is really strange sometimes', he thought, perhaps, recalling last night's conversation. "Anyway let it be", he shrugged, "the cab could be here any minute". He finished his Maggi and gulped the coffee as quickly as possible and hurried to get ready.

***

It was almost four when he boarded his cab, "bhaiya can you turn the AC on for a few minutes please", he said to the driver while making himself comfortable on the front seat beside him. "Hii Aarav", one of his cab mate said in a professional tone, not looking happy with the idea of AC being turned on. "Oh! hii", Aarav replied, "Aaa.. just for a few minutes", he smiled, pointing towards the AC. Then plugged in his earphone and closed his eyes.

"Ghnnnn…ghnnnn", the phone was on vibration mode, he usually kept it in that mode as often as he could. It was a message from Ada, '2.35 is morning for u ha?' A big smile floated across his face as he started typing the reply, 'forgot tht owl ass story?'

Ada: hehe…sry!! cal cntr persn☺

Aarav: so done wid ur practicals??

Ada: yup…jst came out of the boring practl room! Whr r u?

Aarav: in the cab … on my way to borin ofc!!

Ada: borin?? I thot cal cntr is fun!!

Aarav: wat fun! It's jst trainin ol day … sry nit!! clg is fun … nt ofc!!

Ada: and wat abt sexy grls … ha☺

Aarav: ya thr r … bt jst watching thm is no fun … unless u do …

Ada: hanky panky☺???

Aarav: haha … ya!!

Ada: keep tryin … my well wshes r wid u☺

Aarav: thnk u!! So ur'e heading back to hostl … or hav sm othr plans??

Ada: hostel yaar … ppl here r nt tht happenin☹

Aarav: it's in the clg premises … ur hostel??

Ada: no across the road … a little ahd!!

Aarav: hey wat hapnd wid tht projct??

Ada: my team got 85☺!! u rmmbr thngs … thts nice☺

Aarav: I usd to hav a real gud memry … beer ruined it ol☺

Ada: hehe … wat we had yesterday.. ws beer??

Aarav: no tht ws vodka … beer is difrnt!!

Ada: we'll hav beer nxt time … k!!

Aarav: k and isn't it strange … a person frm Goa can't differentiate drinks!!

Ada: hehe … my uncle used to drink … stole it frm his bottle jst a few times … thts it!!

Aarav: k … so an amateur!! btw wat r u wearin tdy??

Ada: yup!! y do u wanna knw tht☺?

Aarav: jst lyk tht … wanna visualize u in a btr manr while chatng

Ada: blck jeans … pink top and white jackt!!

Aarav: wow!! u mst b lukin cute!!

Ada: u thnk so? Thnk u☺ ... wat bout u??

Aarav: black trousr and sea green shrt ... bth formal ... and blck jackt

Ada: clrs gud ... but y formal??

Aarav: it's mnday ... so formal.

Ada: is thr a drs code in ur ofc??

Aarav: no ... bt in corporate ... u shud wear formals on weekdays and casuals on weekends

Ada: Oh!...u lyk it??..I mean u look gud in casuals ...

Aarav: no ... bt atlst during trainin we gotta follow it☹

Ada: u sd ths is ur last week of trainin ... rit?

Aarav: yup ... thn we'll hit the floor an' start takin calls

Ada: wat do thy train u for??...cal takin skills??

Aarav: yup and the process trainin as well

Ada: k ... bt y do thy train at such odd time!!

Aarav: to make us habituatd of the normal wrkin hours!! I hv rchd ofc ... u rchd ur hostel??

Ada: no ...at a nearby grocery store wid my frnd rupali ... wl rch in 20 mins.

Aarav: alrit ... hv fun!! I'm gonna hav to go inside!! Bye

Ada: ok ... bye ... tc☺

"Don't know whats gonna happen in the final assessment on Friday", sitting in the cafeteria for dinner, Neil said to Aarav, who was lost in his own thoughts. "Oye, Rocco!!" Neil raised his voice.

"What?" Aarav looked at him.

"Nothing, who is she?" Neil jerked his brows.

"Who?"

"The one you're thinking about", he smiled. "Is it the metro gal?"

Aarav returned a mild smile.

"I knew it", Neil shook his head mischievously, "is she good?"

"Ya she is good, quite straight forward, lively and most importantly, honest", a shy smile conjugated the statement.

"Oye what smile! Now I know the reason for your changed behaviour".

"Oh just shut up."

"You can't hide it from me saale".

"Two people flunked in the assessment from the previous batch and they were fired". Aarav knew how to get him off a particular track.

"Really?" Neil sounded nervous.

"Yup", Aarav said while looking at his cell. He was thinking about texting her. "Studying??" he wrote and sent it across, giving into the temptation.

"And what about the telephonic round?" Neil asked

"You stumble and you are out", Aarav actually loved doing this with him.

"Not really...ws thinkin abt u only", was her instant reply.

"Me?☺ Why?" he answered, without caring to listen to what Neil was saying.

"Y shd I tel u?...thts my lil secret☺!! Hws trainin goin on?" Pat came the reply.

"Secret?...hw bout a dairy milk☺??...it's dinner break nw...in the cafeteria", his smile almost touched the laughing gesture, while writing this message.

Ada: hehe...my weapon angst me!! Ws thinkin abt the way u talk...ur smile...ur eyes...ufff!!

Aarav: r u falling in love wid me☺??

Ada: Nooo!! ths is jst liking...fr ur kind infrmatn☺!! Whats for dinner??

Aarav: beans...dal...rice...chapati and iceream! U had ur dinner??

Ada: beans … ewww!! icecream wow!! Ya we get it srvd at 9 everyday!!

Aarav: y r u grls so crazy abt choclts and icecreams??

Ada: don knw … y r u boys so crazy abt sutta an ol??

"Abe O!!" Aarav heard Neil's voice.

"What?" he jerked his brows, still looking into his cell phone.

"Who's that?"

"Metro gal", he said slowly and typed a reply, "valid point!! So wats gonna be the topic of tday's gossip??"

"Rocco!!" Aarav looked towards him, "you're finished", Neil said pretending a throat cut with his fingers. Aarav smiled and dived into his phone again.

***

THREE MONTHS LATER

Ada: Wow!! Is that a promotion??

Aarav: no-o-o!! jst a portfolio change…level-2…u cn say!!

Ada: k…bt I still need a party!!

Aarav: saali party khor insaan☺!!…did you evr treat me…wen u topped the interns??

Ada: hehe…evr heard of a persn throwin party fr clearin interns? And btw I alwys give u dairymilk wenevr we meet!!

Aarav: thts the fee fr showin u places…as per the deal three mnths bak…remembr??

Ada: huh!! K-a-n-j-o-o-o-s!!

Aarav: luk who's talkin☺!! alrit jst one truffle cake…k!!

Ada: wow!! Luv u luv u luv u☺

Aarav: gt lost!! I don need ur luv…save it fr ur dreamboy!! Btw hws ur preparation goin fr ur semester exams??

Ada: still a long way to go yaar☹…I havn't compltd even once and rupali is revising☹

Aarav: rupali…haiiii!!! hw is she??

Ada: saale dash hai tu ek numbr ka!!

Aarav: dash…beep…say watevr u want to…bt pls tel hr ..hw mch I ms hr☺

Ada: we r goin fr shoppin tomorw☺

Aarav: shopping??? R u serious?? Jst 5 more days left fr ur semester exams…

Ada: so wat?? A lil refreshment does no harm☺

Aarav: shall I come…

Ada: fr wat?? To tel hr hw mch u ms hr?? gt lost…it's a grls day out☺

Aarav: pls yaar…tomorw is my off.

Ada: ya I knw tht… bt u hav been wrkin fr the last six days… take some rest!!

Aarav: thts k… I can manage!! Bt u tel me… want me to come??

Ada: dying to see u☺

Aarav: hehe… I knew it! thts y u tld me the plan… ha☺!! an listen don die… bcz… u die..I die!!

Ada: shut up!! Save these cheap lines fr ur shayna☺… when is she gonna be back btw??

Aarav: In a week or so!! Listn… managr's around.. I'll call you tomorw… k… bye!!

Ada: k… an stop ths habit of textng while at wrk… or u'll gt fired smday… bye!!

Aarav: fire can't harm me… I'm already so hot☺

Ada: hehe… go see ur face in a mirror!!

Aarav: I'll see it in ur eyes tomrw☺

Ada: gt lost!! :-)

***

"I've reached, in front of the levis outlet, where are you guys?", talking over his phone, all wet in sweat, Aarav looked a little harassed being a part of that endless crowd at the Sarojini nagar market. "Rupali is clearing the bills for her purchase, we'll be there in five minutes", Ada was almost shouting, perhaps they were at a denser populated area and hence a noisy end. "Okay", a smile floated on his face. Her voice did it everytime.
"What happened hottie?" Perhaps she sensed his weariness.

"The sun's hot, I'm not."

"Get yourself something to drink", she giggled, "just there", she added and hung up.

He bought a bottle of water, drank the half of it in a go and streamed the rest on his head. "Aaahh!" It relaxed him. He opened his eyes, some of the people around were staring at him; induction cooling themselves or thinking of him as a maniac, he didn't care. He shook his head and the water droplets sprinkled off his hair. He then brushed them back with his fingers which added an extra shade of shine to it.

While he was checking out his face in the side view mirror of a bike parked in front of a no-parking board, he felt a mild punch on his back. "Ouch!" he cried and turned, rubbing the hit part with his hand. It was Ada, black jeans with sleeveless purple top, matching earrings and hairs tied for a trendy side pony, she looked beautiful as always. "Hiiiii", she hugged him. A couple of seconds later, her face was right in front of his. He touched her nose with his fist, "how are you?" He was smiling. "Good", so was she. They kept looking at each other until bespectacled Rupali's throat clearing sound distracted them. "Hey Rupali", Aarav shook hands with her. Ada was still smiling.

"Look what you have done to yourself", Ada said, holding a part of his wet shirt like a dead cockroach. He raised his face and signaled towards the scorching sun.

"So how's work?" Rupali marked her presence again.

"Good, and your studies? Ada told me you're revising". She smiled in return. "This dumbo hasn't even completed, and where's my Dairymilk?" he hit her softly at the back of her head.

"I ate it", she tittered. They kept strolling down the market like the others.

"Wanna go to a restaurant or something, you must be hungry?" Ada asked after a while.

"Yaa ", he nodded.

***

"One medium Mexican green wave and one medium Gourmet", Ada smiled as she placed the order at the counter of Domino's. Aarav and Rupali were standing quietly beside, watching her. Rupali was okay with any of the hand tossed and Aarav was not allowed to say anything in her pizza matter. "And make it cheese burst", she added and turned towards them with almost all the front teeth in picture; as if she just won the grand slam. Aarav moved towards her with his hand in his pocket, trying to pull out his wallet. "Keep it in, it's my turn", she warned him. "But..." Her stern gaze didn't let him speak.

***

"Why do you keep a record of turns?" Aarav said, while the three of them pulled their share from the pizza, like hungry lions do with the dead gazelle.

"What's the problem?" Ada replied while looking at the garnish on the piece of Mexican green wave in her hand.

"You guys are students, I'm working", he widened his eyes, with a 'that's-why' look.

"So what, pocket money is also like monthly paycheck", Ada said while looking at Rupali, who nodded in agreement. "And you are not my boyfriend", she swung her eyes back towards Aarav with a mouthful of pizza.

He kept looking at her for a few seconds, "thank god... I'm not", he said slowly while pouring himself some coke. Ada threw a sachet of oregano at his face. "Look, that's why I'm thankful to God", he said looking towards Rupali, who smiled in return.

"So, done with shopping?" he asked Rupali, in an attempt to make her feel comfortable.

"Ya", she said with a gentle smile.

"But I'm not", Ada intervened.

"Really?" he was looking at the numerous polybags on the chair beside her.

"It's all hers", she bared her teeth playfully. Aarav kept looking at her but didn't repeat his word - his eyes did it this time. "Okay these three are mine, but just one more top, please", she tilted her head on one side. The searing weather and the crowd outside tickled his nerves but he smiled, which could easily be considered as a 'yes'. This gesture of hers was his weakness and perhaps she knew it, as she exploited it quite often.

***

"Two hundred", she said after a complete inspection of the top she intended to buy and a side discussion with Rupali. Aarav stood silent on her left with folded arms like a bodyguard and Rupali was on her right holding those polybags, like a junior counselor, giving her wise tips in between.

"No less than three hundred", the shopkeeper replied sternly. Ada and Rupali went on a serious business meeting once again. Aarav was still the silent spectator. "Two thirty", Ada said and placed the lemon colour top on the pile of other tops.

She will look really cute in this, Aarav thought but said nothing as he was asked not to. Ada looked at him. "What?" He shrugged. She shook her head, "nothing, come lets go", she said, while taking half the polybags from Rupali. "That was already so cheap, just three hundred", Aarav wanted an explanation after they had moved a little ahead of that stall. "Madam, two fifty", the voice of that shopkeeper was clear. A minute later a new polybag joined the community of the existing ones. Ada smiled looking at Aarav and then winked, "got it?" she said raising her brows.

"All right", he said casually, but was actually impressed by their bargaining skills, "so what's next?" He added.

"You got those sunglasses replaced?" Ada asked after a couple seconds.

"No", he replied.

"So lets go to Rajaouri then, it's already been a month, you got the receipt na?"

"Yup."

"I'm heading back to hostel", Rupali said.

"It's just two thirty now, why so early?" Ada complained and Aarav nodded in agreement.

"Just a little tired", she replied slowly. "And what about you?" Aarav looked towards Ada.

"I'm fine."

"Okay."

"Hey pani puri!!", Ada shouted looking at a road side vendor with small colorful hoardings hanging all around his stall, written clearly in hindi, "dilli aspesal chat."

*****

54

"Any idea how unhygienic that was," Aarav pointed out, while the three of them were walking towards the main road.

"Shopping's incomplete without pani puri," Ada smiled shaking her head in a childish manner. Rupali was smiling. Clearly, she agreed with her. *Girls will be girls,* he thought with a forced sigh.

"So when are we gonna meet again?" he turned towards Rupali, who looked busy with her hair clutcher.

"Let the exams finish, then there's a lo-o-ong vacation", she smiled. Ada remained silent.

"Hmmm", was the only sound out of his mouth. Ada was still silent.

"Auto!" Aarav called as one passed by. It stopped a little ahead.

"Kalkaji", he said to the driver.

"Call me if you get late", Rupali said to Ada, while she got inside the auto with all the polybags along.

"No, I'll be in time."

"Bye Aarav", Rupali shook hands with him.

"Bye", he smiled.

"And text me once you reach hostel", Ada said, just as the auto started moving. Rupali nodded.

***

The centralized air conditioned, state of the art Shopper's stop at Rajaouri seemed more like heaven after almost an hour long journey in auto in the intolerable heat on the roads amidst Delhi's ceaseless traffic. The relief was clearly visible on their faces but they still felt exhausted. "Cold drink?" Aarav asked her, wiping a drop of sweat below her eyes. "No, first thing first", she said.

"We purchased a pair of goggles last month, but returned it a week later as there was a defect, we were promised a replacement", she said to the guy on the other side of the counter, while Aarav forwarded the receipt pressed between his fingers and the desk. "Sure ma'am", the guy answered decently. He took the receipt, sprinted to speak to his colleague or perhaps the manager for a minute and then came back.

"Ma'am if you want the same model, I'm sorry, but it might take another week or so".

"That's what you said last time as well", Aarav seemed a little angry.

"I'm really sorry about that sir but that model is still out of stock."

"This is bullshit", Aarav wanted to add something else but Ada pressed his hand and took the lead, "So what now?"

"Give me one more minute", he excused himself in the same tamed decent manner.

Ada looked towards Aarav, "what's wrong with you?" He closed his eyes and turned his face away.

"Ma'am, either you can get a refund or if you want, there's a complete new range of eye gears." The guy was back.

She swayed her eyes from that guy to Aarav, with a smile on her face, "we would like to try", she said.

"Wow this one looks great!" she said loudly, as Aarav tried another one from the new range, making people around to turn towards them. Aarav swung his head around and found some of their expressions in agreement with her, especially the fairer sex. He then looked towards Ada, who didn't seem to care much about others. With a puppy face, she remarked, "O my Ranbeer Kapoor!" and punched his belly with a naughty smile, making him smile as well. The guy on the other side of the counter smiled with them.

***

"What's with you?" Ada asked with a half smile on her face from across the small pan pizza and two large cold drinks. They were sitting at the most secluded corner of Pizza Hut.

"Nothing", Aarav said slowly while stirring his cold drink with a straw.

"I know it's about the month long vacation after exams", she smiled but rather seemed sad herself. Aarav looked at her face for few seconds but said nothing.
"Look, if you'll behave like this, I'm gonna have to take it as love", she

said it in a theatrical way, swaying the straw in her hand artfully. Aarav couldn't control his laughter.

"Finally!" she sighed.

"Yaar, it's one long month!" he sighed, "who am I gonna chat with, while getting bored at office?"

"But we can still chat," she shrugged.

"You'll be busy with your family, don't wanna disturb you."

"So you are actually worried about your entertainment ha?"

"What else?" he faked a smile, taking a sip of his drink.

"There are so many girls in your office plus a girlfriend, I don't think there's lack of entertainment in your life."

"Naah", he shook his head with a smile, "they don't match your skills." She smiled with pride, he smiled back but it didn't last long. They kept looking into each others eyes, struggling what to say next. "Anything else?" Coincidently a waitress came to their rescue. "No, thank you", Ada smiled.

"So, looking forward to a good performance report this month?" she flipped the topic, perhaps to get away from her emotions. "Hope so." He kept the answer short as he pulled his ringing phone out of his pocket. "Hey Neil; no at Rajouri; in a couple hours, is everything okay; alright", is all she heard him saying.

"What happened?" she asked after he disconnected the call.

"It was Neil, sounded tensed".

"Is he coming down to your place?"

"Ya, he said so".

"Shall I go back then?"

"No, I bought some time" Aarav looked thoughtful.

"Let's go for a walk", he said while finishing his drink in a go. "Excuse me", he waved at a waiter.

"Yes sir".

"One Truffle cake and bill please", Aarav smiled looking at Ada during the early part of his sentence.

"That would be a take away."

"Ya, I know", he said. The waiter rushed to fulfil the request.

"So you remembered?" Ada actually seemed happy. "Ya… how can I forget this stupid pizza hut surprise of yours?" He smiled. She smiled back; this time it lasted.

***

Race Course metro station. Leaned against the side glass of the last seat of the last compartment, with his eyes closed and earphones on, he didn't care to hear the automated announcement. He put his hand on his pocket again to check the dairy milk, it was intact. Her cute smiling face, while she gave it to him just before taking the violet line metro, flashed in his mind, making him smile too. 'Just friends is not what it is'. He opened his eyes to respond to the vibration of his phone that hindered his thought process. It was her message; the smile stretched "jst got out of kalkaji metro station…whr hv u rchd?" It said. "Take an auto frm there…I'm abt to rch", he typed and clicked send. "k…an' lsten I have to buy gfts for Jenny aunty and Peter uncle…aftr the last exam", she texted back. "alrit I'll take a day off…an' txt me once u rch hostel", he replied. Three smileys flashed on his cell's screen within seconds.

***

"Neil, I have reached my house, where are you?" he called Neil while taking the stairs up to his one bed room flat on the top floor of that three storey building. "Are you on the stairs?" Neil's voice was withdrawn. "ya…", Aarav frowned. "Come up, I'm outside your flat."

"Really?" Aarav hurried himself up the first floor. As he reached his flat, he saw Neil sitting on the stairs outside his flat, "Hey Hunter!!" Aarav hugged him. Neil smiled tiredly.

"What's wrong man, why aren't you coming to office for the last two days, and this, beard and all?" Aarav acted joyous, to lighten up his mood. Neil looked at him with painful eyes for a while, "you have got beer?"

***

Neil was sitting on a cane chair in the balcony with his legs pressed against the wall of the room and shorts-clad Aarav looked comfortable

58

on the floor, leaning against the railing. Water droplets on the two recently opened chilled beer bottles, between them, shone in the moonlight. They remained silent in that slow warm wind which felt better than the artificial one inside the concrete walls.

"Life sucks!" 650ml of beer finally triggered Neil's trachea. Aarav remained silent in an attempt to let him vent.

"So how much got credited in your account this month?" Neil said after a while.

"Fifty eight thousand"

"Good, almost the same, but I'm gonna beat you next time", he faked a smile.

"What exactly is the problem?" Aarav asked as he lighted a cigarette.

"Sakshi", Neil sighed heavily. Aarav passed the cigarette to him.

***

"So in one line, her parents want her to get married to a settled guy, which according to them, you're not", Aarav summarised his twenty minute long story.

"Ya...I mean I'm just a useless piece of meat with a fucking guitar hanging around my neck", he said in a shattered voice.

"And this job?" Aarav said slowly, pressing his shoulder.

"Hah! An incentive based call centre job?" he looked into Aarav's eyes, which had no answers.

"And whats her take on this?"

"She says she loves me."

"Man, you sing so well, I'm sure you gonna be a big shot one day", Aarav made another attempt to pacify him. But only saw those watery eyes which Neil failed to hide in the darkness. "I have got two more bottles in my fridge", Aarav went inside the room. 'Rolled tear often reduces the pain.'

***

"You are making the right use of your fridge ha?" Neil smiled on seeing him back in the balcony with beer bottles. Aarav was right, he did feel better.

"So how's your girlfriend?" Neil turned towards Aarav after cleaning the tip of the bottle, who with curled brows seemed confused. "I'm talking about Shayna; saale you'll keep two and you will stay confused like this". They both burst into laughter.

"She is good, probably will be back around 15th", Aarav answered his question, still laughing intermittently.

"Of June?" Neil was also laughing, but the poor eyes still couldn't hide his pain.

"Ya … in the next ten days."

"And what about your metro gal?" he had a questioning smile on his face, brows moving up and down.

"Met today", Aarav said, taking a sip, to avoid eye contact.

"Behanchoo."

Neil was back!!

***

"We should have ordered it", Aarav said while looking at the fried rice look-alike thing they cooked. "This is good man, why to pay five hundred to any stupid eatery, when we can do it ourselves," Neil replied. Aarav widened his eyes looking thoughtfully at the dinner. "You often behave like a millionaire. Save money or one day somebody will reject your marriage proposal as well," added Neil. Aarav smiled at his blab.

"And by the way, who are you gonna marry? Shayna who is in love with you for the last six years, or Ada who has never even said the magical words?" Neil seemed to be on fire today. Aarav shrugged in ignorance.

"You better get it clear then", Neil said putting some rice in his mouth.

"Day after tomorrow there's an in house party that our manager is throwing, are you coming?" Aarav said.

"Don't feel like", Neil made a face.

"We need our rockstar, and you know what, you should be thankful to Sakshi's parents. In this painful visage, you actually look like a rockstar."

"Behanchoo."

"C'mon Hunter, you need some refreshment, at least think of the sexy girls of our team, they'll be in mini skirts" Aarav posed making a wild gesture. A big smile sprouted on Neil's face.

Mini skirts always bring one on boys' faces, regardless of their situation.

***

"Everything else changed but you're still the same", he said looking softly at India Gate. He raised his head, dark brown eyes cringed to travel its height, "you seem shorter… aah! The skyscrapers all around must be the reason", he smiled.

As he walked towards the garden area on the left, he felt her presence. 'This is the place where we met for our last date', he said to her in his mind. He had been talking to her like this for the last twenty five years. 'Everything around here is special, the stones you touched, the flowers you smelled, the air you breathed'. He closed his eyes and took a long breath, 'maybe they are not the same anymore, but they still remind me of every single bit of you, very badly', he wiped the wet eye lashes.

'Aah! There', he found the green colored metal bench under the Gulmohar tree, which appeared older, just like him. He cleaned the dry leaves on the bench and sat on it.

The sun was about to set and the scattered lights off the Gate's edges reflected back in his eyes. He pulled out his cell from his pocket to see the time, "still an hour", he said slowly and closed his eyes.

"Beta don't be shy, make yourself at home", Shayna's mother said for the third time. The designer sofa he was seated on, in the big drawing room of their three bedroom apartment in the posh Vasant Vihar area, couldn't actually make him comfortable. "Sure aunty", he smiled. She went back to the kitchen.

Shayna came a little closer on finding themselves alone in the room, "what are you doing?" Aarav smiled.

"Trying to make optimum use of the situation", she replied flirtily. He looked at her with a gentle smile; red evening gown, open hair, all fallen on one shoulder and carbon framed glasses, "Mumbai has made you classy … ha". She shrugged with a hint of pride in her expression.

"So how was it?" Aarav picked up the glass of water kept in front of him.

"Good, five events in three months, two of them international, The J's is growing".

"Great!! So finally you're making it big", he kept the glass back on the sparkling table.

It's Jaspreet kaur, not me", she said slowly, "But we will, when we start our own business", she added, turning her eyes back to him.

"Hmmm…"

"What hmmm? Think about it", she tucked his hair behind his ear, "hey, I have got a gift for you", she stood up and rushed to her bedroom.

He looked around the room. It looked more cluttered than the last time, with added antique looking mirrors, designer lamps and fake paintings. The vibration of his cell diverted his attention. He took it out to read the message he just received. It was from Ada. "papr wnt well … eight more days … dying to c u☺". He saw his reflection in the mirror on the front wall, it had a smile.

"Aaru", happy Shayna was back in the room with a packet in her hand.

"This is from Rahul Ajmera's collection, I got it for very less, just twelve thousand", she said as he pulled a tie out of the packet.

"This is good, but why did you spend…" he couldn't complete as she kissed him. "it will look very good on you", she justified with a loving smile.

"Okay keep it with you and bring it along when you come to my house next time", he kept the tie back in the packet. She made a face. "I don't like carrying things, you know that", he explained. She twisted her lips sideways.

"Keep visiting beta, it's your own home", Shayna's mother patted his shoulder. "Sure aunty", he said and looked towards Shayna, "bye", he added.

"Go with him, walk him upto the road", her mother said to her.

As they reached the main gate of the apartment, Aarav saw a fat bald man in blazing pink shirt, jeans and sports shoes walking towards them with a big smile on his even bigger face. Only a second later did he realize that it was her Dad. He had met him a few times. The banner in their office, Shayna showed him last time, flashed in his mind. "Gupta properties, sale, purchase, renting", it said with his photo at the left end. 'He has grown fatter', he thought.

"Hello Aarav, how are you?" he said.

"I'm good, thanks". He replied formally.

"And your father? Make us meet him sometime, we look up to his success".

"Sure" Aarav said with the same formal tone.

"Dad", Shayna frowned, "Mom's waiting for you".

"Alright, take care son and keep showing up", he patted his back. Aarav smiled weakly in return.

"So how are things at work?" she asked as they started walking towards the main road.

"Good!"

A sudden gush of wind caused the dense trees on both sides of the silent colony road to dance in a naturally distinct, beautiful way. Birds returning to their nests chirped at their own fixed intervals.

"I'll come to your house very soon, we'll have lunch together", she held his hand, her fingers tangled between his, "I missed you", she said slowly and tightened her grip. He looked at her, the wet eyes glittered gracefully in the street lamps.

***

Slippers, Capri and the lemon top which she had so furiously bargained for; she looked cute like a doll and happier than the underprivileged children outside the Rithala metro station she was buying ice bars for. He saw her ten minutes ago, up from the stairs and since then has been watching her, giggling, laughing and jumping with those children. 'Your smile is so re al that it makes the world a happier place'. He could have watched her for some more time. 'But from tomorrow I won't be able to see you for one long month', he thought and walked down the stairs towards her.

"Why don't you adopt them", he was right behind her, with his hands in his pocket. "hiiiiiiiiiiiii!!!" she screamed, making him nervous for a moment and hugged him. He smiled with a sigh. The children still surrounded them. "You look beautiful in his top?" he looked at her holding both her shoulders, "you didn't say anything that day... but I know you liked it", she smiled.

"Let's take a riksha", he suggested.

"Byeee", she said cutely to the children. Some responded with a waving hand, others still relishing the ice bar she bought them. They walked towards the road to hire a riksha. "Metro Walk", Aarav said to the riksha puller, who quickly took the driving seat and signaled to hop on. "Uncle, one rupee", one of the children, pulled his sleeve. Aarav turned towards him. A boy of about five years with running nose was looking at him. "Saale uncle!" Aarav scolded him. Ada burst into laughter, "who asked you to put on formals?" She said still laughing in her own typical fashion. She took out a five rupee coin from her purse and gave to it to the child, who ran away with it, without even thanking her.

"So how was the paper?" he asked as they were walking towards the main entrance of Metro Walk shopping mall. "Great! you know what, three questions were out of syllabus, but still we….." she babbled in her mesmerising voice till they reached the main entrance of the mall. Aarav listened to her without actually comprehending, *I don't need to, your voice is so sweet*, he smiled to himself.

The spacious, open to sky Metro Walk, with an artificial lake at the centre is one of its kind. They kept strolling for about an hour. "Have you planned the gift?" he asked after they completed the fourth round around the main building. "Ya, perfume for Peter uncle and stole for Jenny aunty", she said confidently. "Let's go to Pantaloons then", he said.

***

After an hour of rigorous and confused shopping, they were sitting on a bench at the lake side. Aarav had a bottle of cold drink in his hand while Ada had both the gifts. She had opted for sun glasses for Peter uncle and a pair of ear rings for Jenny aunty instead of the pre-decided ones. "Are they good?" she asked him, looking at the gifts. He turned towards her, widened his eyes, inhaled a deep breath and took the gifts from her hand, "meri maa, they are damn good", he said and kept it in her purse. She giggled.

"Done with packing?" he asked, taking a sip of cold drink, after a few minutes.

"No, I'll do it tonight"

"Wanna have something to eat?"

"Naah"

"What time are you leaving for station tomorrow?"

"Around two"

"When are you…" he stopped as she kept her hand on his shoulder. He looked towards her, her innocent eyes wanted to say something, "what?" he asked slowly. "Stop playing KBC", she laughed.

"I have booked the return ticket for 24th July, and will be back here on 25th morning", she took out a train ticket from her purse and handed it to him with a smile. "But you said the sessions were gonna start from August the sixth, why so early?" he frowned, but seemed glad looking at the ticket.

"We have to find a house, that's why."

"What's wrong with the hostel?" he returned her ticket.

"You haven't ever seen it, its so-o-o boring."

"Ya you told me about this shifting plan once, so it's decided ha?" he looked happy with her decision.

"Yup, we will be out of that jail and rent a flat, I'm so excited about that", she shook her head with a smile.

"We?" he frowned.

"Ya, me and Rupali", she had that it's-so-obvious expression.

"Okay, and where?" he looked towards her.

"Umm… haven't decided yet, but near college, may be", she shrugged.

"Got the permission from home?"

"Peter uncle may object, but I'm sure Jenny aunty is gonna convince him for my happiness", she smiled.

"We'll decorate it with paints and artificial money plants", her words brought a smile on his face. For the next twenty minutes she explained her interior designing plans. He kept listening, looking into her imaginative eyes. "And I'll invite you for dinner the first day", she looked towards him.

"Dinner?" he smiled, "do you even know how to cook or you're gonna order pizzas?"

"I can cook fish", she widened her eyes in mock anger.

"Fish? Really? And where did you learn that?" he smiled.

She went silent for a while, "I remember, my mother used to cook it for my father", she said after a while, picking up a pebble from the graveled floor.

"You never talk about your parents, where are they?"

"They are with your mother, in heaven", she said after a while and threw the pebble in the lake. The waves on the water resembled the movement of his heart. He held her chin and turned her face towards him. It was calm; her eyes were red, but there were no traces of tears - he hugged her.

***

"This is your fifth month on the floor and I believe each and every one of you is able to contrive a statement clever enough to handle any of the consumer's objections, right?", the potent voice of divisional manager, Rahul Vaish, had the nineteen other heads in the board room nodding once again, excluding Aarav's, who was lost in his own sheer anxiety, so much so that neither the valuable tips of Mr. Vaish nor the silly, muttered comments of Neil, reached his ears. *Every passing minute seems like hours*, he thought, taking his cell out slowly from his pocket, to see the time again. It was 12:05 a.m. *Still two hours to log off and then three more*, he sighed and closed his eyes to curb his impatience. No matter how many times you see the watch, time travels at its own fixed speed.

The exclusive meeting on the usual 'do's and dont's in collections' lasted for another hour. "Alright guys that's all for today, get back to work and happy collections", Mr Vaish concluded the one sided conversation. Twenty exhausted collection experts made their way out through the only door of the board room, some thanking Mr Vaish for his motivational speech.

"Come on, lets go for a *sutta*", Neil said to Aarav as they reached the lobby.

"Okay", Aarav shrugged. They headed their way to 'jitte da dhaba'.

"I don't understand what these assholes are upto. Every single day they have to conduct a fucking meeting and then they question our percentage to goal", Neil didn't even care whether Aarav was listening to him. "I'm gonna talk about this with Mr Director, he is a sensible person, I'm sure..."

"Tea?" Aarav interrupted unintentionally, as they reached the dhaba.

"They make such horrible tea, even my urine must taste better", he said looking at the innocent vendor.

"Bhaiya two tea and two marlboro light", Aarav placed the order.

"And don't make it in just water, like last time, put some milk as well", Neil said loudly.

"You spoke to Sakshi?" Aarav knew his tousled love life is the cause behind his uncouth behavior.

"Ya, things are still the same", Neil said putting the cigarette in between his lips.

"Don't worry, just a matter of time", Aarav said. Neil sighed heavily, throwing up his hands in the air.

"Sir, your tea", the vendor called Aarav, making every possible attempt to avoid the angry young man, Neil. "Easy, it's hot", Aarav said to Neil as he handed him a cup of tea.

"Hey Neil", a small sized guy wearing a large sized t-shirt and a baseball cap, placed his hand on Neil's shoulder. Aarav had noticed him many a times on the floor, flirting around with every approachable girl.

"Hey Tucker", Neil gave him a firm hand shake, "this is Aarav". He introduced him to the guy. "Hii I'm Sumit", the guy said enthusiastically. "How's collections man?" He turned towards Neil, asking the most common question around. "Fucked up", Neil replied with the most common answer.

After a couple of minutes of random chat, Sumit came straight to the point, "man, can you lend me your room for an hour tomorrow?"

Neil kept looking at him for a while, "bro, my room mate will be home", he replied, faking a sorry expression.

"Oh!" Sumit looked thoughtful, may be thinking of other options. "Alright, not a problem, see ya", he patted his shoulder and walked away, "by the way we are going to club 18 after logoff, wanna come along?" he asked loudly from a distance. Neil looked towards Aarav, who had been a silent spectator all this while.

"What?" Aarav shrugged.

"Let's go man, for a change", Neil said, "Tucker, I'll call you after logoff", and gave him an assurance without taking one from Aarav.

"But I have to go somewhere", Aarav said.

"What time?"

"Six in the morning".

"Not a problem, we'll get out from there by five".

***

"You guys stay silent, I'll negotiate and try to make it fifteen hundred a person", after parking his car, Sumit was giving necessary instructions to Neil, Aarav and his two other friends, while they were walking out of the parking area. "Fifteen hundred is just the entry fee?" Neil inquired. "No you'll get coupons worth the same amount, which can be exchanged for beverages in there. Aarav looked least interested in the disco venture, 'but it would help me pass another two hours', he thought, looking at the time; it was 2:55 a.m.

"Hey Aarav bhai", an oversized bouncer warmly greeted him, "how are you?" Aarav tried to recall his name but couldn't. The bouncer didn't seem to mind. "Long time ha?" he smiled. "Ya", Aarav returned one.

"Please", the bouncer signaled towards the main entrance, after taking a thousand a person as entry fee.

"You know him?" impressed Sumit asked loudly, amidst the very loud music.

"Ya, I used to come here, during college time", Aarav yelled his answer. Sumit nodded with lips bent down thoughtfully, "see you around", he patted Aarav's shoulder and disappeared in the crowd. His two friends had already made their way towards the dance floor, with their drinks in their hand.

"What do you wanna have?" Neil asked, mostly in sign language.

"Anything, but not too strong, and lets go upstairs", Aarav shouted bringing his mouth close to Neil's ears.

Aarav and Neil sat comfortably on the couch with a small tipple of whiskey in their hand. "Downstairs, it's too noisy", Neil said while offering a cigarette to Aarav. "I didn't know you have such good contacts at places like this", he added. "I used to be a party animal", Aarav smiled while lighting up the cigarette.

Girls dressed up in shiny short clothes kept moving around purposefully through the over drunk crowd and cigarette smoke. Suddenly the music stopped and the DJ changed the track. People on the dance floor went crazy as the title track of 'Dabang' rolled up. Neil made a face at their taste of music. Aarav smiled, uninterested, "this is club 18", he said loudly, as the music reached the extreme decibel level.

They took around forty minutes to finish their drink. "I'll get some more", Neil said, pointing towards the empty glasses.

"Okay, but it would be my last", Aarav informed.

"Mine as well", Neil replied and stood up from his seat.

"Neil!!" a loud voice from behind made them turn around. "Hey Neil" They saw Sumit coming towards them. He looked heavily drunk, holding the hand of a scantily dressed girl, around three inches taller to him. "You got a *sutta*?" he asked. Neil took out the packet and gave him one. "And one for my girlfriend please", he smiled, taking another one from the packet.

"Hah, typical Tucker's one night girlfriend", Neil said after Sumit had walked away.

"Why do you guys call him Tucker?"

"His alias name on the floor is Carl Tucker"

Aarav raised his brows, "fucker would have been better", he said.

Neil burst out into laughter, "I'll get the drinks", he said, making his way towards the bar counter.

***

After about two hours of their respective drinking, dancing and some other sessions, the five of them stood leaning against Sumit's car, at a roadside tea stall, for the final smoking session. It was still dark.

"Alright guys, see ya", Aarav said, throwing the cigarette, after the last puff. "Where do you wanna go, I'll drop you?" Sumit offered. "No thanks, I'll manage", Aarav smiled, shook hands with each of them and crossed the road. On the divider, he heard Neil's voice, "where are you going by the way?" He turned towards him and smiled, "Nizamuddin railway station."

***

He was walking down the desolated service lane as the auto driver had dropped him at the main road making an excuse of gas refill, a ten minute walking distance from the railway station.

First sun rays falling on his face, through the capering leaves of surrounding trees, added to its radiance. The early morning breeze, fluttering the collar of his shirt, made him close his eyes for a moment to feel the fragrance it brought with itself. *Although it's been a long time since I have seen a fine morning, but never one like this. What was so special about this morning?*

Apart from just a few tea vendors and some beggars, getting ready for work, the platform number six of Nizamuddin railway station seemed like an abandoned lifeless property. He made himself comfortable on a bench near a tea stall, under the sheltered area, as the rays of the ascending sun felt considerably hot now. He was awake since last evening and his whole body was urging him to get a good sleep, but his eyes had something else to say. He kept looking frequently at the time in the digital clock hanging from the roof of the shelter. To him, it seemed to change from 06:46 to 06:47, in days. "Babuji, tea?" He turned his face towards the voice. An emaciated old man with only traces of flesh and watery dead eyes, had a kettle and some plastic cups in his hands. "Ya, sure", he signaled for one and the quivering hands followed the request. "Is this platform always like this?" Aarav asked while giving him a ten rupee note, which brought some shine in his eyes. "Yes, most of the time it's like this only", he fished out a five rupee coin from the pocket of his torn kurta and offered it to Aarav. "No that's okay, keep it", Aarav said. The old man looked into his eyes, "I earn whatever I can with hard work, babuji", he said with a smile and handed him the coin. Aarav kept looking at the glaze of self respect on his pale face. "What time is the train gonna arrive?" he managed to ask after a while.

"Which one?"

"Goa express" A smile floated across his face.

"In fifteen minutes", the old man said and moved ahead.

***

The strong arrival whistle of the much awaited Goa express, finally brought life back on the platform. Even before the train halted, he located compartment number B2, cloaked behind a staircase pillar. He kept watching the people coming out of the compartment, after the train had stopped. An old aunty stepped out first, then a bald man, perhaps her son, then a thin guy with two heavy suitcases. His heart was beating at double the pace, a sweet little girl with her parents; his heart wouldn't listen to him, then a fat man with fat glasses. As she got down, Aarav saw her, the doubled up pace of his heart suddenly dropped down to zero. Magenta colored top, white stole, black jeans and slippers with a big back pack stooping her under its weight. Ada looked extremely beautiful.

He couldn't stop smiling. He walked behind the exhausted and tardy Ada. 'Glad or Happy', are not the words competent enough to describe his feelings at her sight. *What is it then?* Deep down his very self, an unacknowledged thought, laid the inevitable fact as an answer to this perplexed question. He increased his pace and came closer, but was still behind her, "madam, porter?" he mimicked a rustic tone in a different

71

voice. "No", she replied slowly, without even looking back and kept walking. He held her bag, "Madam please", and pulled her. "Are you crazy!!" she turned back. Aarav was standing with his tilted head and a big smile.

"Hiiiiiiiiiiii!!" Ada's usual vociferous horrifying greeting filled the environment for a couple of seconds.

***

Aarav took a detailed look of the not-so-bad, neat and clean food court they were in. Washed table cloths, decorated walls and dimmed lights were not exactly what he expected from the name 'Railway Jalpan Grih'. Apart from an old couple, silently relishing a single, double sized dosa at the other end, it was just the two of them. 'Dosa? So early in the morning', he thought and turned towards Ada, who was busy cleaning her face with tissue papers. He kept watching her, giving her a smile every two seconds. Glasses, some forks, spoons and five crumpled tissue papers lay on the table between the two smiling faces.

"So how come you are here?" Ada finally uttered, after a non-stop smile that lasted for about fifteen minutes. "You showed me the ticket that day, it had the arrival time and the compartment number", he arched his brows.

"But in any chat or call you never told me that you were coming to receive me", she smiled again.

"I'm full of surprises", he circled his hand in self praise. She smiled to appreciateand took out another tissue from handbag.

"God!! How many times are you gonna wipe it, it's already so clean, fresh and beaut… " an extra screen of her mesmerizing charm, perhaps brought by his own extol, captured his senses for a moment, " … ifull", he completed after a while. A mild wave of shyness travelled across her face. She smiled and kept the tissue back in the bag, but couldn't break the eye contact. He kept looking at her, *I shouldn't be staring at her like this*, he thought, but he couldn't help it. "What can I get for you sir?" a sudden voice in south Indian accent, brought them back to present. Aarav turned his face, a thin dark waiter with thick bushy moustache was casting a tamed smile. They should be trained for timings as well.

Aarav started slipping his finger on the menu card, "aa…grilled sandwich, coffee and…" "Only masala dosa, at this time sir", the guy interrupted, in his typical accent. Aarav looked at him and the dramatic change in his expression had Ada bursting into laughter.

***

"How is your uncle's joint pain?" Aarav asked from across a big Dosa in between. "Not so good, he stays at home, most of the time", she said.

"So Jenny aunty is handling the library?"

"Yup", she nodded.

"Is she able to do it alone, at this age?" he looked at her, while struggling with the dosa with his spoon and fork.

"What do you mean at this age, she is hardly forty five", she frowned while looking into her phone, "do you have network in your cell? I need to call Rupali".

"Is she also coming today, for the mission house hunt?" he said smilingly, passing her the phone.

"No tomorrow morning", she smiled back and dialed her number, "can't reach her", she made a face and returned his phone.

"Are you gonna be alone in that hostel today?" he looked serious.

"No, I'm sure other girls would be there". He nodded in relief at her answer. *God! I have started caring for her.* He thought to himself.

"How's your office, met your target?" Ada's voice interrupted his thought.

"Ha?" he creased his brows, puzzled. "Office!" she said a little louder.

"Yaa, good", he yawned slightly, perhaps the word 'office' was the reason.

"You have been awake all night, na?"

"Hmmm…" he nodded like a child.

"Who asked you to come here?" she looked angry. *Has she also started caring for me?* He kept looking at her cute angry face.

***

At two thirty, his alarm woke him up, as usual. "It's my week off idiot!" He raised his head from the pillow and yelled at his innocent phone, turned the alarm off and fell back. *Is everything okay at her hostel?* was the first thought of his conscious state. He dialed her number.

"All set?" He asked as she received his call in just two rings. His tone was still sleepy.

"No", she said slowly.

"Why, what happened?"

"Nobody is here, it's locked", she said.

"What!!" he yelled.

"Ya, I called my warden, she said it will not be opened before the first of August."

"Where are you now?"

"At the kalkaji bus stop."

"God! You are at a bus stop, why didn't you call me stupid?" he sounded really angry.

"Didn't want to wake you up", she said cutely. A smile sprouted on his face at her answer and the anger vanished, "I haven't seen a girl as dumb as you, take an auto right now and come to my house", he said after a while.

"Do I need to tell just Green Park", she said slowly.

"Add Reliance fresh, near the metro station."

"Okay".

"You are really crazy", he laughed, "what if I had woken up at ten in the night?"

"Then I would have killed you", she almost cried.

***

In his shorts and a t-shirt, he was standing in front of the Reliance fresh store. Every passing auto with somebody else inside was augmenting his uneasiness. "whr hv u rchd?" He typed his fourth message, after three calls, in the last half an hour and sent it to Ada.

"drvr sd jst abt to rch", came her reply, after ten seconds. "Cal me once u rch the metro statn", he typed and before he could have sent it, he got her call. He received it in just half a ring, "hey I have reached the metro station, left turn na?" she asked. "Yes", he replied. At the same moment, he saw an auto at the turn, with a part of her white stole, fluttering out in the air. A smile took over his anxiety.

"You have got all the sea side stones in your bag?" Aarav said pulling her backpack's strap, up his shoulder, as they took the stairs to his apartment. "Give it to me", she giggled.

He shook his head, "it's okay," he smiled, "so how was the experience?"

"What experience?" she simpered.

"Your six hours stay at the bus stop", he mimicked her smile.

"Haha, good", she replied. He looked at her, the jaded, cute little face was not in agreement with her answer. Every single fiber of his being, felt like hiding her in his chest, with his arms around her.

"Why? You met any handsome stranger?" he raised his brows.

"Hah! Look at my hair and face, you think any handsome guy would look at me?" she pulled a few strands of her hair in front, "It has gotten so dirty!" she exclaimed. He smiled at her obliviousness.

"Hey! This is cuter than you described it", she yelled as he opened the door of his flat. Although he cleaned it up for her visit, but still didn't expect this reaction. "You like it?" He had that, are-you-sure, expression on his face. "Yaaa", she seemed so happy and excited, "and the balcony?" she looked at him with beaming eyes. He walked with her to the other end of his room and opened the door to his park facing balcony. "Wow!" she said slowly and clung to his arm. The extra beats of his heart, at her touch, substantiated the pious warmth they share. He turned towards her, the tired eyes looked innocent as always and the sweat drenched face seemed to be the most beautiful one he had ever seen. He touched her nose with his fist, "don't ever do it again", he said softly, after a while. She kept looking into his eyes with her watery ones and then kept her head on his chest. Even the hot wind felt like heaven. He put his arms around her.

"Ada", he whispered in her ear, after around five minutes.

She hummed like a child and sunk herself deeper in his chest.

"You really need a bath, your hair's stinking", he laughed out loud. She pushed and punched him on his belly, "saale kutte", she laughed but tears on her lashes were clear as pearls.

"I'll get lunch packed, while you get changed", he said, wiping her eyes.

***

"Madam, here's your fried rice, chicken chilly and momos", he smiled and raised the poly bag in his hand, as Ada opened the door. Wet open hair, peach colored t-shirt melting in the glow of her skin and a white knee length skirt; she looked like something divine. "Wow! After how many years have you taken a bath?" he entered the room and kept the packet on the table. She hit him on his shoulder and sank on the sofa, curling her legs up, underneath her, "I'm so hungry", she said while opening the packet. "And I'm so tired", he said and sprawled beside her.

"Did you tell Jenny aunty about this?" he said.

"No, didn't want to worry them, just told her that I have reached safely", she swirled a momo in the dip and gave it to him. "And you spoke to Rupali?" he asked while adjusting the hot momo in his mouth.

"No, her cell is out of reach since morning."

"Haaa… she betrayed you", he closely imitated a girlish style, with his hand in front of his mouth.

"Shut up, there must be a reason", she grinned and pinched him on his thighs, "how's your manager by the way?" she said while opening the packet of fried rice and chicken.

"That homo… still the same lazy ass, we have changed his alias name from Sam Baker to Sam 'Bekaar'." His intonation made her burst into laughter. He looked towards her, that childish natural laugh, delighting even the most basic part of his composition.

"And your friend Hunter?" she said after a while, still laughing, "Did you two watch Desi Boys together?"

He nodded, "ya, on the very first week off", he said smilingly.

"How is he?"

"Umm... fine, trying to cope with the situation", he said softly, putting a spoon full of rice in his mouth.

"He loves Sakshi a lot, doesn't he?"

He nodded in reply, "love, at times, assesses toughly."

"So what, anything for life", she said.

He turned towards her, with brows mildly cringed at her answer.

"Love after all... is life", she shrugged in justification.

The ring tone of her phone interrupted their serious discussion on an upcoming bollywood flick. She picked the cell from the table, "It's Rupali", she received it with a smile. "Hey Rupali, where are you, I have been..." she frowned and looked at the display, as the call got disconnected. She got down from the sofa, went to the other end and opened the balcony door, guessing the problem could be of connection. "Hey, it has turned dark outside!!" she swung her head towards Aarav, who also seemed surprised at the outdoor view. He looked at the wall clock behind him, it said 8:10 a.m. "Madam, we have been talking for the last three hours", he said and picked up the empty poly bags and plates from the table and walked towards the kitchen.

"Spoke to her, she broke her phone last night, didn't have my number stored anywhere else so called up after getting it fixed", she said in a single breath, as she entered the kitchen after ten minutes.

"I thought she ran away with a guy", he smiled as he swirled a spoon in the sauce pan he was making coffee in.

"Shut up! She is not like that", she protested, leaning against the cooking shelf.

"Why, is she a lesbo?" he brought his face closer to hers and quickly moved his brows up and down, twice. She pinched on his hand, "saale tu hoga gay", she said grinding her teeth together. "She will come to Delhi by tomorrow afternoon and will stay at her sister's's place in Rohini. She wants me to stay with her", she said slowly after a couple of seconds.

"So you'll leave me tomorrow?" he said in a baby voice, making a sad pouting face.

"Hehe... yeah baby, we have to find our new house before the month ends", she pulled his cheeks with her hands and smiled looking into his eyes. He saw a streak of pain in her, attempting-to-smile eyes, perhaps at the thought of leaving him and wondered if it's there in his own as well. *Why are you becoming almost as critically important as the air I breathe*, he thought, *Is it love?* he heard a question within himself, in his own voice. "The coffee's boiling!!" her clamor left that question unanswered.

With the coffee tumbler in their hands, they stood close to each other in the balcony, silent in the silvery moonlight. The hot evening, less as compared to the ones lately, could be considered as just better, but with the expressions on their faces, seemed like it was magically pleasant. While keeping and picking the tumbler up from the railing, his fingers lingered around her's, causing those strange reflexes. Ada closed her eyes and inhaled a deep breath, to smell the watered mud of the park in front or to curb those unforeseen desires, within her. He couldn't understand in the blurred light. "Are you drunk?" he laughed at her sudden yoga posture. She turned towards him with a smile and stared strangely for a moment, "you know what, let's get drunk", she chirped after a while.

"No!" he blatantly refused.

She brought her face in front of his and rolled her eyes mischievously, "Let's booze baibiyee!!" she pushed him with her waist, with her hands up in the air, holding the coffee mug. He burst out into laughter, "beer or vodka?" he said, jerking his brows slyly.

***

"Ewww!! it's bitter than vodka", sitting on the bed on her huckle, upstraight, she cringed her eyes as she shook her face,stucking her tongue out, after taking a sip of beer from the glass Aarav had just poured for her. "I already told you, now keep eating something", he shrugged and smiled from the sofa he had pulled beside the bed. The fluctuating light of the computer, they had played a movie on, was the only one light apart from the palemoonlight through the balcony. The shadows of swinging branches of the eucalyptus tree outside covered almost half the floor, from the balcony end. He kept smiling, looking at the comical changes in her facial expression, with every sip of the beer, while she was watching her favorite movie, 'Aawarapan.'

"Is aawarapan ka bojh ab aor nahi saha jata", Emraan Hashmi said to the leading lady of the movie, leaning against a car, struggling with his life, with bullets in his chest. He saw tears rolling down her cheek, "are you okay?" He asked controlling his laughter, but somewhere in his heart he felt, a part of it twisting, on seeing her cry. She threw the pillow from her lap to the other end of the bed, "yaa", she said, wiping her tears and still trying to smile, "I don't wanna see him dying", she added and fell on the pillow.

The computer was now behind her and she was facing Aarav, who looked smug on the sofa. Two glasses, three empty bottles of beer and lots of crumpled packets of snacks, lay on the table in front; he had his legs sprawled on. "You really like this movie, don't you?" he said, looking at her. She squeezed her hands between her cheek and the pillow and folded her legs a little, looked into his eyes and let out a huge sigh, "the love story of this movie," she said after a while. She looked like a child, who had cried all evening for her toy and is now ready for sleep. "Somehow it reminds me of my parents", she added a little later, eyes staring at nothingness, as if she was completely lost in her memories. The movie ended and there was an absolute silence in the room. He straightened his back slowly, to sit upright, but said nothing.

"I remember my mother's smiling face, watching my father, offering prayers", her mesmerizing voice pierced the silence, after a few minutes.

"How did they get married?" He paused for a second, I mean arranged or…"

She kept looking into his eager eyes, "they met at a medical conference in Bangalore."

"They were doctors!"

"Ya both of them", she smiled, "my mom said that she fell in love with my dad the day she saw him. His simplicity touched her to her core. Six months later, he was transferred to Goa, in the same hospital my mother was employed with. They came closer and started meeting after work. Sometime later, my father proposed to her for marriage, she said yes and they tied the knot."

"No family objections?"

"Ya, Jenny aunty says that initially Peter uncle was not happy with my Mom's decision, she was just twenty three then", she smiled, "but for the happiness of his sister, whom he had brought up like his child, he finally agreed."

"And your father's family?"

"He was an orphan, raised in a small foster home in Mumbai but he took permission from the care taker of that foster home, whom he respected like his father. He was the one who arranged funds for his studies. I met him a few times. Dad used to take us to Mumbai for his blessings", she slipped out a hand from under her cheek and wiped her face, "aren't you tired sitting on that sofa?"

"No, I'm okay", he smiled to hide his killing urge to hold her face in his palms and kiss her eyes until every single trace of pain is drained out.

"C'mon I won't rape you", she shook her head, moving aside to make some space for him. Her retort made him laugh. He heaved himself up from the sofa, walked upto the bed and lay down beside her.

"You know I miss them a lot", her voice sank.

He kept looking at the ceiling, "how did they die?" He asked carefully, after a while.

"I remember it was Friday; a rainy Friday. I was at school. Jenny aunty came around the recess time and took me to the hospital, saying that Mom met with a road accident. When we reached there, I saw Peter uncle crying and my dad standing silently in a corner. On seeing me, Peter uncle hugged me and said that she died half an hour ago. I was just eight then". Ada turned towards Aarav, held his palm and pressed it between her face and shoulder, "everybody cried, but I never saw my dad crying, he almost stopped speaking after her death and three months later, he died of a heart attack", she sunk her face, deeper in his palm, "their love was so deep", she said drowsily after a while. He felt the brush of her closing wet eyelashes against his palm. He turned towards her and kept looking at her innocent face, till sleep shrouded his senses.

***

It was not until Shayna patted his wrist that he remembered he was with her. "Would you please stop playing that stupid game in your phone?" She said as he looked at her. He was actually not interested in listening to her take on the designs and defects of the dresses the models showcased in the fashion show they just came out of.

"I'm thankful you took the day off, but if you can't even talk to me, it's useless", she said seriously.

"It's not like that, I got this game just yesterday, so you know...", he said with a smile and kept the phone on the table in between them, "what were you saying?" he added, curling his mouth in apology.

"Forget it", she made a face and took a sip of her coffee, "you know how hard it is for me to be with you", she said firmly after a while.

"And why is it so?" he almost laughed.

She kept looking at him for some time, "I am in love with a person who doesn't even care about my feelings."

"It's not like that Shay..."

"What is it then?" She interrupted, "do you even remember; when was the last time you took me for shopping?"

He laughed, "Now I can't afford the brands you wear". She looked at him and smiled a second later at his answer, or perhaps at her own question.

"Okay forget shopping, today we would be together for the entire evening, a movie first and then a romantic dinner", she said excitedly, so loud that it got several heads turned towards them in the coffee shop they were in. She gritted her teeth and cringed her eyes. He smiled.

"Where?" He asked.

"Umm... connaught place", she said slowly.

***

The orange evening sunlight reflecting from the dark green grasses of the central park, was adding an aroma of romance to the influences. "You remember how often we used to come here during college days", she said slowly, putting her hand on his.

"Hmmm…" He was looking at the group of kids playing volleyball.

"We were so happy at that time, no worries about career and all", she said.

"Is there any worry now?" he looked towards her.

"I'm worried about you Aaru."

"Me?" He frowned.

"You don't take anything seriously, your real profession, your love, your family", she stumbled.

"Not again Shay, please."

"Alright but think about it, there's nothing this call centre job will fetch you", she said and kept her head on his shoulder, "I love you", she whispered a minute later and closed her eyes.

"Why do you love me?" He didn't want to ask that, but still he did.

She stayed silent for a while, "because you are my future", she said slowly, "I wanna be with you always", and pressed his hand firmly.

"What's the show time?" she said after a long silence. "6:30 p.m., I guess", he replied and took out the movie tickets from his pocket to take a look at the timing. "Yes, 6:30 p.m. We should go now, it's already 6:10 a.m.", he said and as they stood up, her phone rang. Aarav saw her walking away as she received the call.

"It was Jaspreet, she is throwing a party at her new bunglow for a contract we just got." she said smilingly to Aarav as she returned after disconnecting the call.

"So?"

"These are the parties where you get a chance to make contacts", she curled her brows, "so, we are going to the party", she smiled a second later.

He made a sound by pressing his tongue against the palate, "I'm not coming to any party."

"Shut up", she said and pulled his hand, "let's go".

"Shay, I'm not coming", he said firmly this time, "you can go if you want to", he added.

"Are you sure?" she asked. He nodded in reply.

"Alright, get me a cab then", she made a sad face, but her eyes were not in line with her expression.

***

He tore the movie tickets as her taxi moved. *Hah, wanna be with you always*, he imitated her tone and smiled vaguely, *you are actually much more confused than me*, he said to her in his mind, turned around and made his way to a cigarette shop.

"Marlboro light", he said to the shopkeeper who had his stall in front of a wall full of pamphlets saying; work from home, massage parlor, lose weight and such. "Eight rupees", shopkeeper said loudly and gave him the cigarette. As he was lighting it, he managed to read a few more, but the one which grabbed his attention was, 'to-let services'. *Did they find a flat?* he thought, took his phone out of his pocket and dialed Ada's number.

"Hii", she sounded a little tensed.

"What's up ma'am?"

"Aarav, we didn't get any flat, classes are starting day after tomorrow."

"What about the one you saw yesterday?" he said.

"They asked for too much of security money, and we have searched almost the entire extension, nothing suits our finances", she sounded like a child.

"Why didn't you call me then, I thought you guys would have finalized it by now?"

"You took a day off to be with your girlfriend, didn't want to disturb you".

"Stop being so modest, learn to exploit friends", he laughed and heard her laughing as well. "Now listen, I don't know anything about Kalkaji, but I can arrange something in Hauz Khas, it wouldn't be too far from your college and from my house as well", a smile spread across his face, at the later part of the sentence.

"Let me talk to Rupali", she said.

"Alright, I'll talk to a few contacts of mine, if something positive turns up, I'll text you, if Rupali is okay with Hauz Khas, come and finalize it today itself, okay?"

***

"No late night parties, no smoking and no wastage of water", around sixty years old, Mr Singh, said firmly; seated on his arm chair, in his drawing cum bed room, looking at Rupali and Ada. "And rent on time", he put forward his final condition, on which the three of them nodded in rhyme.

"It's a two room set, you can take a look, third floor", he said and handed the keys to Rupali.

"Beta have some tea first", Mrs Singh, came in with a tray with three cups of tea and some snacks on it.

"Not for me?" Mr Singh exclaimed. Stupid Ada burst into laughter. "Are you crazy?" Aarav muttered, nudging her with his shoulder.

"He already had two cups since evening", Mrs Singh said smilingly, looking towards Ada, who smiled innocently in return.

"They are so-o-o cute", Ada said slowly to Aarav. "Ya he looks like Manmohan Singh," he whispered in her ear. She kept both her hands on her mouth, taking loud deep breaths, to control her laughing mania.

"Are you two... boyfriend and girlfriend?" Mrs Singh said, looking towards them with a sweet smile on her face. Her unexpected question suddenly increased the warmth of his blood, his heartbeat accelerated so fast that he could actually feel them. He looked towards Ada, who had a thin shy smile on her face. "No", she said to Mrs Singh and turned towards Aarav, "just friends", she added slowly, but it sounded like a question to him, for which he, by any virtue, had no answer.

"Oh! But you two look so cute and compatible together," she shrugged slightly, "you know, made for each other kinds", Mrs Singh spoke her heart out, leaving them both on a silent note.

***

"So finally you guys got it, I need a party", he smiled looking towards Ada and Rupali, while walking down the colony road, towards the main one.

"Sure, tomorrow we will shift here by evening, how about dinner?" Rupali said.

"Tomorrow I'll be at work, but on next week off I'll definitely come here for the fish she promised", he looked towards Ada, who gave a brief smile in return. He then quickly switched his gaze back to Rupali. Mrs. Singh's sober utterance had landed them in this awkward situation. "There are lots of buses running between the places", he launched himself in relevant conversation.

"My sister has a scooty, which she seldom uses, she said we can use it", Rupali said smilingly.

"What else could be better!" he exclaimed, throwing his hands in air, "and if you guys have any problem, I'm just a call away."

"So you'll come here only when we face any problem?" Ada said with a slightly sad voice, after a long time. Her question brought a deep smile on his face. "And whenever I'll get to know that you guys have cooked something tasty, I will barge in without a warning", he smiled gleefully, looking into her big black eyes.

"We'll also come to your place whenever we'll get to know you've got momos", she giggled.

"And I'll also come for a shower, whenever there is a shortage of water in my building."

"Whenever we have to watch a movie", she tilted her head.

"Whenever I need a scooty ride."

"Whenever we have to booze."

"Sali piyakkad", he pushed her with his shoulder.

"Tu hoga piyakkad", she pushed him back.

Rupali kept smiling at the quick resumption of their 'compatibility'.

***

The half moon and the stars peeped intermittently through the floating clouds. The cold autumn wind up the hill top, breezing through the trees, made sounds as if hushing to maintain the existing quietness. The silence of that cold night of Rishikesh, quite far from the crowded and noisy Delhi, had Aarav meet himself after a long time.

Sitting on a rock, at a secluded edge, with his hands curled close to his chest, Aarav kept looking into the darkness, with his thoughts whirling in his mind. *There is something that keeps me so happy these days, there is something that has added meaning to this restless life, and I'm missing that something so intolerably here*, he took out his cell phone from his pocket and opened the gallery. Scrolling down the images of Rishikesh, he stopped at Ada's; trying to hide her face, but her cute smile was caught in the picture, he took when they went for boating at Purana Quila, just a few days ago. He couldn't move his eyes from the display, until Neil's voice harshly hit his eardrum, "Coffee is ready!" Aarav turned towards the camps behind and saw Neil coming towards him with two tumblers in his hands. Just then, a sudden vibration of his phone pulled his attention back; it was a message from Ada, "It's alrdy been two days, come bck soon☺." He smiled mildly looking into the phone, *perhaps 'that something' is you*, he said slowly, slipping his thumb softly against the phone's screen.

"The trip's over madam, we'll be heading back tomorrow morning", he typed and sent it across as reply, after a couple of seconds. "Here's coffee", Neil sat beside him.

"Who was it?" Neil inquired, looking towards his phone, passing him a tumbler.

"Ada", he replied with a thin smile on his face.

Neil curled his mouth in confusion, "what's your actual scene with Ada?"

"I don't know", Aarav bent his lips down, "there is something about her, that attracts me, very intensely, every single word she speaks, makes its way to the bottom of my heart, every single moment she is with me, delights me to my core", he shrugged slightly, "I just like her a lot."

"Do you love her?" Neil asked sharply.

"What!" Aarav laughed, "are you crazy?"

"Just say yes or no," he asked flatly.

His laughter was taken over by a confused portrait, "no", he said thoughtfully after a while.

"Are you asking me?"

"I'm telling you", Aarav said firmly with a smile on his face, "anyway just let it be" he jerked his shoulder, "is everybody else asleep?"

"Ya, most of them", Neil said looking towards the camps, "the water rafting was really tiring."

"But it was fun."

"Really", Neil nodded in agreement, "next time we will go to Nainital."

"*Sutta*?" Aarav took out his packet of cigarette.

"At least these vacations slack the stress", Neil continued, as he took a cigarette.

"And what stress do you have?" Aarav smiled.

Neil widened his eyes thoughtfully, "a lot man!!" he sighed.

"Like?"

Neil kept looking at him for a while, "like this sword edge job, like my studies, like my love…" he inhaled a deep breath, "…like my life" he said slowly exhaling the same breath out.

"What exactly are you doing this MBA entrance preparation for?"

"So that I can get a job that is good enough to convince Sakshi's parents", he said as he took the lighter from Aarav, "but it seems it's not gonna be of any use", he added slowly.

"Why?"

"Because her parents have already seen a guy", he said, as he lighted his cigarette, "some banker... She said"

"Why doesn't she refuse at once?"

"It's not easy to handle parental pressure", Neil said looking straight in his eyes, "but she says she is trying her best".

"Don't worry, things are gonna be alright", Aarav said, "and these troubles, actually are the spices of love", he added as he took a puff of his cigarette. Neil smiled in return.

"What time are we gonna leave for Delhi tomorrow?" Aarav asked after a while.

"Around eight may be."

"So late!"

"What's the hurry, it's our off tomorrow" Neil questioned.

He opened his mouth, but words came out a little later, "I think I'm missing Delhi."

***

As soon as Aarav entered his room, he threw his hand bag on the sofa and sprawled on his bed, with his phone in his hand and fingers ready to dial her number. But before he could, to his surprise, his phone vibrated with her name flashing on the screen. 'What timing, ha!' He smiled and received the call.

"Hello madam", he said with a big smile on his face.

"How was your trip?" Ada chirped.

He could feel the tautness in his face muscles, as his smile stretched to its limit, at her voice. "Good", he said, a couple of seconds later.

"Just good?"

"Yaa, just good", he laughed at his imitation, "had you been along, my answer would have been different", words slipped out his mouth, even before he realized.

"And what would it have been then?" she giggled.

"Awesome!!" he said rather confidently this time and felt the shy silence on the other end.

"What time are you gonna get out of college?" he asked after a while.

"Usual time, around four."

"How about a coffee at Ansal plaza, at five?"

"Are you sure?" she said slowly, "I mean you must be tired."

"It's 11:30 a.m. now, enough time to take rest and just in case I stay asleep you can wake me up", he said.

He could sense a smiling face on the other end and a second later he heard, "Alright."

"Bye then", he smiled.

"Bye", she said and the call got disconnected. He kept the cell on his chest lost in the merriness of the moment and gradually, sleep took over his senses. Strangely, a mild smile stayed intact on his face.

***

Sharp at 4:10 p.m., his phone vibrated, still on his chest. He had not tossed or turned even a bit. He opened his eyes and took a few seconds to gather himself. It was a message from Ada, "wake up kumbhkaran!! :-)." He couldn't resist a smile that accompanied the long yawn. "I'm alrdy awake ... U got out of college?" he typed and sent. His whole body was crying out for a little more rest, but he got down from the bed, his body protested by cramping at various parts, especially his back, yet knowing that his heart was so desirously dying to see her. He picked up his towel, but kept looking at his cell, which was lying on the bed, for her reply. It vibrated in seconds, "I knw my msg woke u up☺ ... nw gt ready ... dyin to see u☺!!" It said, bringing another deep smile on his face. He kept the cell back on the bed, and went for a shower.

***

He entered the Plaza and spotted her standing in the front lawn under a shed, strewing an unimaginably beautiful smile at his sight. He met her just last weekend, but the two days trip to Rishikesh, felt like ages of separation. And now that she was right in front of his eyes, his very soul felt mesmerized with the vision of 'that something' that he missed so much in the last two days. He increased his pace as he saw her walking towards him. Within seconds, there was just a thin layer of air between them, distorted by the fast breaths of two smiling face. He kept looking into her twinkling eyes, unblinked for a while and then touched her nose with his fist, "how are you?" He asked slowly. She nodded and hugged him with all her strength.

"So, how was the college today?" he said taking a sip of his coffee.

"Internals will start in a week or so", she replied sadly in a baby voice, stirring her coffee unnecessarily. It was her signature step whenever she was compelled to do something she did not want to, especially when it came to academics and he loved watching her do that. "Why? Aren't you prepared?" he asked, with a half smile.

She shook her head coyly with her lower lip protruding a little. He felt a grin grow on his face at her countenance. "What is it that's stopping you from studying these days?" he said after a while.

"Don't know", she shrugged, with a shy smile on her cute face. He raised a brow cynically, "have you found your dream boy or what?" He knew the answer would be 'no', but still his heart incited to hear it. He didn't want her to be with anybody else, although he never said he wanted her to be with him - just him and he had nothing to justify this strange feeling of his.

"No-o-o", she smiled as she stretched her answer. He sighed faintly in relief.

"So, are you looking for one?" he asked a little later, looking into his cup of coffee.

"And why do you wanna know that?"

"Just like that", he swayed his gaze back to her.

She smiled into his eyes, "of course I'm looking for one", she said slowly and moved her gaze away, "the one who will make me laugh all the time, whose company will make me feel like I am flying, whose touch will have the power to take away all my pain, who will always be crazy for me."

She looked back towards him, "and I will be equally crazy for him", she simpered.

He felt warm at her answer. He felt as if she was talking about him, "don't you think I fit in there", he said slowly and added a quick laugh to make it sound like a joke. But he saw her freeze, with her sharp black eyes widening a little at his reply and his fake laugh gradually vanished. He wanted to read those black intense eyes and get the answer, but like every time, his own confusion reflected back from them. He quickly swayed his gaze to his coffee, "It's nice, isn't it?" he said. She hummed in reply. For quite some time, there was silence.

"Let's go for a movie", she broke the silence after paying for the coffee.

"And your studies?"

She made a sound pressing her tongue against her palate, "a day is not gonna make any difference", she smiled.

"Alright", he said loudly and stood up from the chair, with a huge grin on his face.

***

He insisted on dropping her home as it was nearly 10:00 p.m.by the time they reached Hauz Khas, after a two and a half hour long romantic movie. They left the auto at the main road and now were walking down the lane to Ada's house. Although it wasn't too late, but there was a peaceful silence around and they preferred not to break it. Every gush of wind was warning about the nearing winter, but the beautiful company he was with had its own distinct warmth.

He kept looking at her glowing face in the faded yellowish street light through the corner of his eyes. Her hand, lingering around his, as they walked, woke a killing urge to tangle her soft fingers firmly in his. But he couldn't gather the courage to hold something that was so close to him yet so far.

***

"Ghnnnnn… ghnnnn." It was the fourth time his phone vibrated in the last five minutes, it was the fourth time he inhaled a quick breath, needing that extra amount of oxygen, to handle the sudden excitement. He looked at the display. It was a message from Neil. Date December 7, time 11:54 p.m. and it was the fourth time he exhaled the air out of his lungs in disappointment. *Why isn't she messaging me, has she forgotten?* He thought as he shrugged slightly and opened the complete message, "hey rocco happy birthday!!" It said.

"Thnks… but it's nt 8th yet", he reverted.

"So wat, wantd to be the frst persn to wish u… even before ur grlfrnds… haha", came his reply in twenty seconds, bringing a mild smile on Aarav's face.

91

Aarav: "u're fourth bro… three ppl alrdy wished…bt u seem so happy…my b'day can't be the reasn."

Neil: Sakshi refused fr the engagement, with that bastard banker☺

Aarav: grt…that buys u anthr chance thn… so what's nxt??

Neil: Chance?? anthr life man!! same thng, whch I'm doin fr the last five mnths…studies…MBA entrance…

Aarav: and no getting back to music??

Neil: at times u hv to dump ur dreams…fr the sake of love.

Aarav: wow hunter…keep up the spirit!!

Neil: jst don't frgt the party man …bye tc!!

The smile on his face was soon taken over by the persisting anxiety. He kept his phone aside and picked up the bottle of water in front. Birthday for him had always been just another day, but he failed to understand the reason for an obscure sensation this year. *Has she fallen asleep? But how could she?* He kept the bottle back on the table, *she kept talking about a surprise, God!! Why am I even thinking so much about it?* He looked at the clock on the wall…one… two… three… he was holding his breath…four…five…'what nonsense am I doing'…six …seven… it struck midnight…eight…nine… and his phone vibrated again. He quickly turned towards it, feeling the same breath surge…he looked at the display…It was Shayna calling… and he exhaled it out in the same disconcert. Whose call was he waiting for then?

"Hey shona, happy birthday, ummaaah!!" she said, as he received the call.

"Thanks Shay", he said slowly, with a thin smile on his face.

"What happened birthday boy, you sound a little jaded?"

"Nothing, just sleepy", he lied.

"Alright go to sleep then, and Mom has asked you to come for lunch tomorrow." she said.

"Okay I'll try."

"No trying shrying, you have to come."

"Alright!!" he sighed in defeat.

"Love you, happy birthday once again, ummaah, bye."

"Bye Shay", he said, disconnected the call and fell on the bed. He didn't want to, but still he looked at the clock. It was ten past twelve now. Every taut muscles, with which he was holding his ardour, loosened. He shook his head a little, *she must have fallen asleep.* He turned off the light, let out a huge sigh and closed his eyes.

Barely five minutes had passed when an unexpected door knock made him open his eyes. *Who could possibly be here at this time?* he thought as he got down from the bed, 'landlord?' 'watchman?' possibilities scrolling down his mind as he walked through the room, 'a friend?' his hand reached the door knob, 'or is it she?' His thought transformed into words, out his mouth, in excitement as he pulled the door open. He was right! Ada was standing in front of him, holding a small cake in her hand with a tiny candle burning on top of it; her head tilted on one side and that out of the world smile on her beautiful face, glowing in the candlelight; "happy birthday", she said softly.

***

"So this was your idea of surprise, ha?" he said, wiping the cream she spread on his cheek. "Yup!!" she said taking a bite of the cake piece from her hand.

"And you took an auto at this odd hour?"

"1 arranged for a pepper spray", she said cutely pointing towards her hand bag, while making herself comfortable on the sofa, curling her legs up.

"A pepper spray? You're crazy", he laughed.

"Don't laugh, I had to take the risk to make it as special as I could", she protruded her lower lip out like a child, "It's your first and last birthday with me", she smiled, but the reflection of her dismal heart, through her cold eyes, felt like a rusty razor infixing deep into his soul. "So you'll go back to Goa after the final semester?" he asked slowly, switching his gaze vaguely to his fingernails, perhaps to avoid eye contact.

"Yaa, Jenny aunty is handling everything alone, plus Peter uncle's health conditions are not often well", she said slowly. "This is not that chilled", he tapped the bottle with his finger twice and sprinted towards the kitchen.

"Stop drinking chilled water, it's December now", she said loudly, looking towards the kitchen. He didn't reply, he couldn't, for he felt being choked at the thought of her leaving Delhi forever.

"Hey I have got something for you", she said, as he came back into the room, with a sham smile on his face. "What?" he said.

"This!!" she pulled out a stuffed monkey toy from her hand bag.

"What is this?"

"This is you", she smiled and gave it to him. Its hairstyle was crafted like his and it was wearing a hand stitched t-shirt with 'I'm hot!!' written on it. The room reverberated with his laughter.

"This is cute, thank you", he said, while keeping it in the glass pane cupboard, where only his special things got a place.

"I'm feeling hungry, you've got Maggi?" she said rubbing her stomach.

"I'll make one", he said and made his way towards the kitchen.

"Wait, wait, wait", she shouted, jumping off the sofa.

"What?" He turned.

"I'll make it", she held his arm.

"Really?" he frowned, "I mean, you have been here so many times, but how come you decided to cook today?"

"Because, it's your birthday", she pulled him towards sofa, "so you sit here like a king and let the slaves do it", she bowed artfully, making him laugh again.

"There's no water in the tap", he heard her voice from the kitchen.

"Keep it open for a while", he crossed his arms close to his chest and kept his legs on the table, perhaps to enjoy the next minute fun.

"Oh!! God!!" He heard her scream, a second later at the sound of rushing water.

***

"Ummm… it was good, Rupali is teaching you to cook, ha", he said, as he kept the spoon in the empty bowl and set himself loose on the sofa, beside her.

"Oh! I forgot, she asked me to wish you a happy birthday on her behalf", she said hitting her forehead with her palm.

"Just wishes, no kisses", he gave a quick smile, looking towards her.

"Saale kutte".

He laughed, "Why didn't she come herself?"

"She is studying".

"And how's your studies going, by the way?"

"Not that good" she said sadly, "I hope my exams go well."

"Just wishing is not gonna work", he nodded, bringing his face close to hers.

"Wish is everything. You don't wish, you don't get", she imitated his nod.

"Then I wish I were the president of America", he said.

"And I wish I were a lead scientist at NASA", her quick reply had both of them laughing.

"Yaa…" she stretched thoughtfully, "these are human greed, not wishes. A real wish is something that gives you real happiness, it comes from within, from your very self", she said after a while.

"Sex?"

"Shut up!" she hit him on his thigh, "you know, deep within every heart, there is at least one wish", she said after a couple seconds, looking into distance, "the wish that gives it a direction, and even the imagination of its fulfillment has the power to bring the deepest of smiles".

He bent his lips down in a frown and nodded thoughtfully, "what's yours?"

"I wanna open an orphanage", she smiled, "and yours?"

"Ummm..", he raised his shoulder, "A café!" he smiled, looking into his imagination, "the most romantic café, serving the most delicious coffee!" his hands were up in the air, trying to describe, "It would be open to sky with lots of shrubs, giving it a look of some sort of a garden", he turned towards her, "and there would be an age limit, no oldies". She burst into laughter, "romance knows no age, stupid".

"Really?" he asked. She nodded, still laughing, with her hands on her mouth.

"Okay so age no bar, but I haven't decided the name yet", he shrugged.

"How about romanti' cafe?" she said after thinking for a few seconds.

"Hmm... that's good, but something exclusive", he shook his hands, and went thoughtful, "Quixotic!!" "Café Quixotic", he said precisely, opening both his hands in front of his face, as if he was actually viewing it.

"Mine is better", she made a face.

He looked at her cute face for a moment, "alright! Romanti' café, happy now?" he threw his hands in the air. She smiled tilting her head on one side.

"And you can come with your dream boy there, if you want to", he said slowly, like a child, looking away from her. Under her magical influence, he often used to get this long lost child, deep within himself, out to play.

She laughed, "and you will welcome us with your wife."

"Wife?" he looked at her, with raised brows, "who's gonna marry a guy like me? No ambition, no career, no money."

"What has money got do with it anyway", she frowned, "and as far as career is concerned, I think you're doing well", she shook her head, "and most importantly you're so-o-o cute."

"Really", he let his expression put a question mark on it.

"Yaa, any girl would love to marry you."

"Why don't you marry me then?" He looked into her eyes, curling his lips into a taunting smile.

She kept looking at him for a while, being intricately thoughtful, "you know what, let's get married", she said bluntly.

"What!!" he laughed. "Yaa", she shrugged, "the world, as we know, will end on December, 21."

"22nd", he corrected.

"Ya whatever, so I don't wanna die without accomplishing my childhood dream of getting married", she smiled.

"What's in it for me?" He smiled.

"Ummm…you'll not die, thinking about your chances of marriage."

"And what if the world dosen't end?" he asked.

"Then we will have a story to tell our grandchildren", she laughed. He kept looking at her stupid gesture, with a deep smile on his face and a jumping heart in his chest, "but I'm a Hindu and you're a Christian, wedding style is gonna be a problem?" He said somberly, perhaps he didn't want to sound as stupidly excited as her.

"Umm… let's follow both of them", she shrugged being thoughtful, "but why leave Muslim style", she looked towards him with a glaze in her eyes, "ya, lets follow all three", she smiled.

"And when?"

She kept her forefinger on her lips and went into some mental calculation. "Next week my exams will start", she tapped her lips twice, "let's do it now", she said slowly.

"When?" Either he didn't hear her, or perhaps just wanted it to be confirmed again.

"Now!!" she smiled.

***

"Ada don't you think, what we are doing is really crazy?" He said while sitting on the floor, cutting some news papers.

"I got it!!" she shouted, looking into her cell phone, and completely ignoring his concern.

"What?"

"The Muslim wedding vows", she looked towards him, "so we now have all the three wedding vows", she tapped her finger on sheets of paper placed on the table. She jotted down the vows by searching on google.

"Write down the Muslim ones as well."

"They are very short, let them be here only", she shook her cell phone, "wow!! Those are really good", she added as she saw the flowers he made from the news papers.

"I'm a NIFT grad, ma'am", he smiled with a hint of pride in it.

"How will you sew it to make garland, Mr. NIFT grad?"

"I bought a needle and thread sometime back", he seemed thoughtful, "must be in the kitchen somewhere."

"You keep needle and thread in kitchen?" she got down from sofa and headed towards kitchen.

"Look in the lower shelf", he shouted.

"Can't find it", he heard her loud voice after a minute.

"Then look in the fridge, egg rack".

"You are impossible, who keeps needles and thread in fridge", she came back into room with the needful material in her hand.

He laughed, "so the garland problem is solved, candle will be the holy fire, what about Muslim and Christian wedding?

"I've got my stole to cover my head for Muslim wedding", she smiled.

"And Christian?"

"We don't need anything for that", she tapped her lips, being thoughtful, "yes Alchohol, to raise the toast, you've got any?"

"No", he nodded.

"Why, you mostly have beer in your fridge"

"Thought not to drink on my birthday", he shrugged slightly.

"Yaa… didn't see any bottle", she made a face, "let it be, we will use water."

"Hold on", he curled his mouth, thinking about something, "I have got cough syrup", he said with a triumphant smile.

***

"I, Ada Maciel, offer myself in marriage and in accordance with the instructions of the Holy Quran and Holy Prophet, peace and blessing be upon him. I pledge, in honesty and with sincerety, to be for you an obedient and faithful wife." She switched her gaze from her cell's display to his eyes. A mystic wave travelled across his whole body, making every single word echo in his mind and melt down through his nerves, directly to his heart.

"That is it?" he said gathering himself, after a couple of seconds.

"Yup, I told you, the Muslim vows that I found on google are short", she said softly, "here's your part", she smiled and passed the phone to him. He saw her fair hand quivering as he took the phone.

"What's wrong?" he said.

"Wedding jitters, perhaps", she said smilingly, inhaling a deep breath.

"Is this gonna be a real one?"

"Of course not", she rolled her eyes, "Instructions say, witnesses and guardian required".

"But it feels like…" he shook his head, '…nothing, shall I read my part". She nodded.

"I, Aarav khanna, offer myself in marriage and in accordance with the instructions of the Holy Quran and Holy Prophet, peace be upon him. I pledge in honesty and with sincerety, to be for you a faithful and helpful husband." There was a complete silence in the room as he finished.

"We are husband and wife now", he said slowly, breaking the ice.

"Congratulations", she said and hugged him. Her heart beats were so fast that he could literally feel them pounding against his chest, "are you okay?" he whispered in her ears. She hummed and tightened her grip, "hey!!" he caressed the back of her head as he heard her drawing deep breaths, "I told you earlier I'm not worth marriage, why crying now?"

She pushed him, wiping the tear on her long lashes and a mild smile on her face.

"Now Hindu style?" he said after a while.

"No, we will go as per increasing vows length order, so next is Christian."

"Alright, so we gonna have to mix a little of cough syrup with water to make our toast", he turned towards kitchen, "No" she said a little loudly.

"What?" he turned around.

"We have to read the vows ourselves, so no alchohol, even if it's cough syrup", she said firmly.

"Why?" he frowned.

"These vows are sacred", she said looking into a distance, as if she had started to understand their meaning, in the real sense.

***

"This is your part", she said and handed him a piece of paper, "and this is mine", she smiled.

"Me first?" he asked innocently.

"Yup!!" she nodded. He kept looking at those joyful eyes, gratifying him thoroughly to the extent of numbness, "read it!!" he heard her voice.

"Ya", he switched his gaze to the sheet in his hand, "Alright, here we go."

"I, Aarav Khanna, take you, Ada Maciel, to be my wedded wife. With deepest joy I receive you into my life that together we may be one. As is Christ to His body, the church, so I will be to you a loving and faithful husband. Always will I perform my headship over you even as Christ does over me, knowing that His Lordship is one of the holiest desires for my life. I promise you my deepest love, my fullest devotion, my tenderest care. I promise I will live first unto God rather than others or even you. I promise that I will lead our lives into a life of faith and hope in Christ Jesus. Ever honoring God's guidance by His spirit through the Word, And so throughout life, no matter what may lie ahead of us, I pledge to you my life as a loving and faithful husband.", he then raised his brows inquiringly.

"That was good", she smiled, "now my turn."

"I, Ada Maciel, take you, Aarav Khanna, to be my wedded husband. With deepest joy I come into my new life with you. As you have pledged to me your life and love, I too happily give you my life, and in confidence submit myself to your headship as to the Lord. As is the church in her relationship to Christ, so I will be to you Aarav khanna, I will live first unto our God and then unto you, loving you, obeying you, caring for you and ever seeking to please you. God has prepared me for you and so I will ever strengthen, help, comfort, and encourage you. Therefore, throughout life, no matter what may be ahead of us, I pledge to you my life as an obedient and faithful wife." she shook herself slightly, shrugging her shoulders. "Congo!!" She said and held out her hand to him.

"What congo?" he seemed serious, "where was that, 'you may now kiss the bride' part?"

She giggled, "Let's do that too."

"Really?" he left his mouth open, rolling his eyes mischievously.

"Yaa", she shrugged, "but here, if you really want to", she tapped her cheek.

***

"I couldn't find who has to be ahead, while taking 'pheres'", she protruded her lower lip out a little.

"That actually has got some meaning, but anyway you stay ahead."

"Alright so read the groom's part and then I'll follow with my part", she instructed. He nodded like an obedient disciple.

'First vow.'

Aarav: My beloved, our bond strengthens by your walking one step with me. You will offer me food and be helpful at all times. I will embrace you and provide for our welfare and happiness and also that of our children.

Ada: I humbly comply with you, my lord. Kindly bestow upon me the responsibility of the household, food and finance. I promise you that I shall carry out all responsibilities towards the welfare of the family and the children."

'Second vow.'

Aarav: My beloved, now you have walked the second step with me. Fill me up with strength and courage so that together we can protect the household and the children.

Ada: My lord, in your sorrows, I shall fill your heart with courage and strength. In your joys, I shall rejoice. I promise you that I will please you at all times with sweet words and take care of the family and the children and you in turn shall love none other but me as your wife.

'Third vow.'

Aarav: My beloved, now you have walked three steps with me. With your presence in my life, our wealth and prosperity are going to grow. I shall look upon all other woman as my sisters. We will educate our children and may they live long.

Ada: My lord, I will love you with single minded devotion as my husband. I will treat all other men as my brothers. My devotion to you will be that of a pure wife. This is my commitment to you.

'Fourth vow.'

Aarav: My beloved, it is a blessing that you have walked four steps with me. Your presence in my life has made it sacred and auspicious. May we be blessed with obedient and noble children and may they live long.

Ada: My lord, I will enrich myself from head to toe with sandalwood paste and fragrance for you. I will serve you and please you in every possible way that I can.

'Fifth vow.'

Aarav: My beloved, now that you have walked five steps with me, you have adorned my life. May god bless you and may our loved ones live long and share in our prosperity.

Ada: My lord, I will share your happiness and grief. With your love in my life, I will trust and honour you. I will fulfill all your wishes.

'Sixth vow.'

Aarav: My beloved, you have filled my heart with happiness by walking six steps with me. May you fill my heart with joy and peace at all times.

Ada: My lord, in all righteous acts, in material prosperity, and in enjoyment of acts approved by the divine, I promise I will stand by you.

'Seventh vow.'

Aarav: My beloved, as you have walked the seven steps with me, our love and friendship is now eternal. We have attained a spiritual union blessed by god. Now you are one with me and I offer my life to you. Our marriage will be for ever!

Ada: My lord, as per the laws of God and the sanctity of the Holy Scriptures, I am your wife now. Whatever promises we made, were made with a pure mind. We will be truthful to each other in all matters and we will love each other forever.

And they exchanged garlands silently.

"I have attended so many marriages, but I never knew the meaning is this deep", he sighed after a minute.

"Wasn't it ..gr..great?" Her voice choked.

"Magical" he said softly.

"You know what, marriage is not a simple love affair, it's an ordeal, and the ordeal is the sacrifice of ego to a relationship in which two becomes one", she said looking into distance.

"You came up with that?" he turned towards her and asked incredulously.

"No, read it on internet", she smiled.

"That was incredible", he rolled his eyes, "anyway let's talk about dowry now."

"Saale, you will give me dowry", she hit him on his shoulder, "hundred dairy milk, hundred truffle cakes and hundred pizzas."

"Where can I apply for divorce", he said seriously with a comical intonation, letting the room fill with her sparkling laughter.

"One thing's left", she said after a while.

"What?"

"The vermilion tradition."

He kept thinking for a few seconds, "Shall I cut my thumb, like heroes in bollywood movies?"

"Shut up!"

"There is no other option though", he shrugged. She looked at him for a while and then dropped her lips down in submission.

"A single drop of blood is enough", he said pinning the needle in his thumb. She turned her face away.

"Ouch!!" he cried softly, "here it is, you're ready?"

As his thumb touched her, she closed her eyes and took a deep breath. He couldn't move his gaze from the radiating thin lines of nervousness and happiness on her elegant face. Something in him drove a deep desire to hold her for a moment, if not forever, "it's done", he said slowly. She opened her black watery eyes that spoke more than her prolonged silence; but like always, he couldn't comprehend. She took his palm in her hand and pressed it between her face and shoulder, "now you're my husband", she said softly.

"And you're my wife", he smiled dotingly.

"Just that, there is no witness", she smiled.

He shook his head, "there is." He held her hand, walked to the other end of the room and opened the balcony door. The earliest, blurred sunlight at the horizon filled half the sky with its devout splendor, "this morning is our witness", he said softly.

***

The first month of the New Year was nearing its end and so was that day. The chilly evening and his cheery mood were just like they had been lately. With all the happiness, excitement and some anxiety reflecting widely in his expressions, he kept strolling in front of Pacific mall, with his cell phone in his hand and his eyes glued to its display.

"whn r u gonna rch here", he typed and sent it after an impatient twenty minutes. Within seconds his phone vibrated. It was from her. "Turn arnd my hansm hubby☺." A big smile sprouted across his face like a smooth wave formed on a still lake at the drop of a pebble. With a usual tickle in the pit of his stomach, he turned around. Ada was walking down the pavement towards him with a big beautiful smile on her face, making all his senses stammer for a moment.

"Hiiii", she said softly as she reached close. He kept looking into her eyes, "you love making me wait, don't you?" he said. She let out a soft laugh. "No", she shrugged. "It's just that, you always reach a little earlier", she said showing him the time in her phone's display, "it's eight now and if you remember, this is what we decided, so I'm on time". He curled his mouth with a hint of admiration in his eyes, perhaps at her quick comeback and touched her nose with his finger. "But it's always better to be early, isn't it? My sweet little wife", he said letting the corners of his lips stretch into a thin smile.

"Ya", she nodded like a child.

His smile stretched wide across his face, "hungry?" He enquired. She nodded again.

***

"Umm... have some more", she said pushing the pan pizza a little towards him. He shook his head, "no I'm full." She shrugged and took a big bite off the one in her hand. He smiled, "how's your diet for pizza so incredibly good?" She smiled, shrugging in her typical fashion with her mouth full of pizza.

He kept looking at her for a while, "you're a cartoon, you know that!"

"Really, you think so?"

He widened his eyes a little, "of course, I know you for almost a year now".

"Hey", she didn't let him complete, "are we gonna celebrate our anniversary?"

"Which anniversary are you interested in celebrating?"

"Umm... first time we saw each other", she rolled her eyes. "Well that's Valentines Day and my birthday, so calls for a big celebration", she said shaking her head childishly, as she fixed her gaze at him, "and the first time we met and … "

"That's it", he said loudly, "no more 'ands' please", he smiled.

"Why?"

"February and March are high seasonality months, so getting leaves would be even more difficult, that's why."

"What's seasonality?" She asked.

"In collections, there are months when chances of account settlement are high", he tried to explain, but on seeing her blank expression, he took a deep breath and said, "in short, I can't promise anything."

She kept looking at him for a while and then picked up the last piece of pizza from the pan, "hah, you and your promises", she said slowly, sprinkling some oregano on it.

"Now you are being a typical wife", he laughed, "any promise that I haven't kept so far?"

She kept looking at him, being acutely thoughtful. She opened her mouth twice, perhaps to say something, but couldn't. "Look, you actually have nothing to complain", he smiled proudly.

"Yes!" she almost shouted, suddenly remembering something.

"What?"

"You promised to take me to disco", she said, widening her eyes.

"When?"

"Now you are being a typical husband, don't even remember your promises", she smiled naughtily, "can you recall our first chat?"

He kept thinking for a while, "Okay, so when do you wanna go?"

She giggled, "When do you wanna take me?" she imitated his tone.

He smiled, "how about today?"

"Hah", she made a face, looking straight in his eyes. He kept on smiling. "Are you serious?" she asked after a while.

"Does it look like I'm not?" he said with a big smile.

"Wow!! Where?" she almost yelled with a broad grin on her face.

"Umm … The stage."

"Great!" she erupted with joy, "lets rock." He burst into laughter, "you are a big cartoon."

***

The night had just started and as expected there were only a few people in the club, which certainly couldn't be considered as 'crowd'. The rotating disc light and the slow music seemed to kick start the night. "So desolated!" she said looking around, exasperated, "in movies, discs are over crowded." He turned towards her, "this is not a movie", he said raising his brow, "this is a night club, and the night's just started."

"But I wanna dance like Preity in kal ho naa ho." She pouted childishly.

He laughed, "Then get drunk like her, first."

She smirked, "beer?"

"No", he made a face, "let's have tequila this time", he smiled.

It was around eleven when they finished their fourth shot of tequila. The night was now darker and the disc brighter, just as expected. She stood up to join the dance floor, "come on", she said tugging him at his elbow. "No", he said flustered, still letting himself be dragged.

A little less under the influence of tequila than being of one another, they kept dancing slowly to the not so slow music, entangled in each other's arm, with a constant thin smile on their faces.

There was something about the moment that made him float in the seventh layer of the sky. He didn't know why but somewhere deep within himself he wanted that time to freeze. The strange feeling that he always had since the first time he saw her, was getting strong enough to let it form into words, but before he could say anything, he heard her murmuring his name.

He held her chin, "what", he asked slowly, raising her face.

"Aarav", she said making every attempt to keep her eyes opened, "my head is spinning like a cartwheel". The pain in her innocent voice twisted his heart, "you don't have to listen to anybody, who asked you to go for the fourth shot?" She smiled slightly, with half opened eyes, "sorry", she said cutely. He kept looking at her, "let's go back, I'll drop you", he said holding her face in his palm, "why didn't you tell me earlier?" he asked, barely managing to keep her on her feet.

"Because you would have said the same thing." He widened his eyes in question. She kept looking into them, "I'll drop you", she said.

He smiled, "Why? What's the problem with that?"

She tightened her grip around him, "because I want to be with you, it feels soooo… good", she sunk her face in his chest.

His smile turned into a big grin, "you still can, but I don't want you to crash down here, we are going to my place, okay."

***

"Thank you very much for walking up the stairs on your own", he said as he let her sit on the sofa and took her arm off his shoulder. "I thought I'll have to carry you in my arms." She smiled faintly as she threw her sandals off her feet. He smiled back. "I'll get you some lemon water", he said and made his way towards the kitchen. He returned after five minutes and he saw her sleeping in her usual childlike position. A soft smile sprouted on his face. He kept the glass on the table and picked up a sheet and a pillow from the bed. "Why are you such a dumbo?" He said as he put the sheet on her. She stirred. He ran his fingers against the softness of her cheeks, upon the jaws and ending at the chin. He gently held her chin in his two fingers as he gazed warmly upon her sleeping face, "and so-o-o cute", he said slowly, pressing the pillow under her head.

"Aarav", she murmured, "I.. love..", were the only words that came out of her mouth. His heart pounded violently. Every single fiber of his being, wanted her to complete the sentence. He settled on the floor, with all the wait in his eyes, but she didn't say it. His earnestness to hear her say them was not more than the biological fatigue that his body felt. He kept his ears concentrated even on the slight unevenness in her breathing, till he dozed off, leaning against the sofa.

***

"Where were you? It's more than ten rings." Aarav said impatiently, as soon as the call was received.

"Hello, jiju."

"Oh! Rupali, hii, where's Ada?" he toned his voice down.

"She is in the shower, getting ready for her fourth date anniversary", she giggled, "how many of them are you guys gonna celebrate, by the way?"

"These are her ideas, I'm just being dragged", he laughed, "once she goes back to Goa, after the final semester, there will be no more dates, no more anniversaries", he felt something pinch his heart, while he maintained the laugh.

"Yaa...", she stretched sadly, "so what time are you gonna be here?"

"Umm... actually, Shayna got promoted yesterday. She is throwing a party, so I might get a little late."

"Oh! My poor jiju, stuck between wife and girlfriend", she laughed.

"How's studies going?" he tried to avoid her blab.

"Good"

"And Ada's?"

"How worried!" She laughed again, "ya she is also studying hard."

"She is my wife after all", he laughed slightly, "okay listen, just tell her I'll be a little late."

"Would you like to give a time?"

"Around eight may be."

"Alright, I will tell her, bye."

"Bye", he smiled.

***

"Hiii, jaaaan", Shayna chirped, as she opened the door. Dressed in black sleeveless trouser suit with abstract lines and some crystals, a silver belt and some designer jewellery, she looked sophisticatedly glamorous.

He stared at her, "hiii", he said slowly with an appreciative smile.

"C'mon in", she pulled him by his hand.

"Hii Aarav!!" a few out of half a dozen people already present in her drawing room greeted in rhyme, as he entered. He waved his hand at the unknown crowd with a fake smile on his face.

"These are my new colleagues, I already told them about you", she said gleefylly and introduced them, "some college friends are also expected", she smiled looking at him after the last intro.

"Really??" he seemed excited, "Who all?"

"Nisha, Ruby and Manish are on their way, perhaps Perry will also join".

"Ruby? Our cutie pie?" he said with a big smile on his face.

"Yaaa, your cutie pie", she imitated him.

***

Sitting on a sofa, in a corner, he watched Shayna and her colleagues, roaming around in her three bedroom apartment, with glasses of cold drinks in their hands, sipping off and on. Their tooth and nail effort to make it look like some page3 party, seemed as feigned as that extra painting and plastic money plants, occupying the left over space on the front wall. Light music on the roll was the only fair attempt.

He took a sip of his drink, picked up a magazine from the table in front and started turning its pages, without caring to read any of the articles.

"You're really a lucky man, Shayna is so-o-o hot", a thin guy with a coarse voice, sprawled on the sofa beside him.

Aarav turned towards him and tried to recall his name, from the introduction.

"Samar, they call me Sam", he said, brushing his colored hair back with his fingers, gauging Aarav's thought.

"Sam", Aarav said in a calm but firm voice, "you are talking about my girlfriend."

"Oou!! I'm sorry if you didn't like it", he raised both his hands in air in surrender, but a foxy smile still lingered on his face. Aarav kept looking at him for a few seconds and then switched his eyes back to the magazine.

"But she never minds, I even praise her curves sometimes", he added after a while. Aarav felt like punching him hard on his face.

"I need some help in the kitchen", Shayna's sugary voice, from the other end of the room stopped him.

"At your service ma'am", Sam sprinted towards her.

Aarav nodded vaguely and pulled out his cell from pocket. *It's 5:30 p.m.*, I'll leave in an hour, he thought and as he kept the phone back in his pocket. The door bell rang. He saw Shayna walking upto the door.

"Heyyy!!!" shouting at the top of their voices, four familiar faces invaded the apartment; Nisha, Manish, Perry and Ruby. A big smile appeared on Aarav's face.

***

"Then I stopped her in the middle of the road and said, I love you", Perry said, sitting on a chair in front of the sofa which was occupied by Manish, Ruby and Aarav.

"Then??" they all asked together with a hint of suspense in their tone.

"Then what, like the previous ones, she also slapped me", he said slowly, with his hand on his cheek, making them burst into crackling laughter.

"Keep on trying Perry, one day success will come to your feet", Ruby said, still laughing intermittently. Perry threw his hands in the air and looked up, "It's all upto Wahe Guru", he sighed.

"It's been a long time", Aarav said slowly to Ruby, "like around…"

"Two years", she completed with a smile, "actually a little more than that".

"But you haven't changed a little, still the chubby kid kindzz", he smiled, "and stop wearing this hair band."

"That's my style", she touched her hair band and then kissed her fingers, "Alia Bhatt copied me", she rolled her eyes. He kept smiling.

"Where are Shayna's parents?" Perry enquired.

"They are out of town, attending a marriage", Aarav said.

"Let's booze then", Perry swayed his gaze through the three of them.

"You better ask Shayna", Manish said.

"Where is she?" Perry looked around.

"She is in that room with Nisha and other friends", Ruby pointed. Perry made way to the signaled room.

"She doesn't have a problem", he smiled as he returned to the drawing room, "come Manish, lets get it arranged", he said and they both walked out.

"So?" Aarav turned towards Ruby, "how are things going?"

"Umm... good", she shrugged slightly, picking up her cold drink from the front table. "You tell, I heard you are working with a call centre these days".

"Yup"

"And did you sort out your problem with your dad?"

"How come you know about it?"

"Shayna", she shrugged.

He shook his head, "no", he said sluggishly after a couple of seconds.

"So, are you never gonna talk to him?" she said looking straight into his eyes.

"Don't know, but not now, atleast", he sighed, "I was fed up of his speeches and taunts", he said slowly, "and you know what, doing every thing on my own actually makes me happy", he added.

"But Shayna must not be happy with this decision of yours."

"Yaa", he nodded, "she told you this?"

"No, just made a guess."

"What made you guess she is not happy with my decision?" he smiled, looking at her, picking up his drink from the table.

"That my friend, you need to figure out yourself."

He went thoughtful for a moment then made a sound pressing his tongue against the palate, "forget it, you tell, made any boyfriend?" he smiled, pushing her with his shoulder.

"Yup", she simpered, "four so far!!"

"Really?" He exclaimed, "but you didn't even have one, during college", he smiled, taking a sip of his drink.

"Because in college I had a big crush on you", she said bluntly. He almost threw up, "what!" he blurted out loud.

"Yes, I was the one who fell in love with you and talked about you with Shayna and all", she looked towards him, "but Shayna was the one who proposed you, even though she was already in a relationship …", she stopped as her phone rang, "yes Mom, I'm at Shayna's place, ya I'll be…", she kept on talking, which Aarav didn't seem to be interested listening to. He picked up the magazine again.

"So where were we?" she turned towards him after fifteen minutes.

"It's beer time!" Perry howled, making an entry with a crate of beer in his hand, before Aarav could have replied.

***

Amidst the loud music, dances and laughter, the flow of beer never stopped.

"That's it, I can't dance any more", Ruby said, trying to hold her breath, "Aarav it's your turn now"

"Are you crazy?" He laughed.

"Come na, shona we'll do it together, like we did at the annual function", Shayna stood up and pulled him by his hand.

"No!" he smiled embarrassingly. "I don't even remember the steps", and slipped his hand out from hers.

"Huh!" she made a face, "C'mon Perry, let's dance", she said.

"O! yaar, dancing with empty stomach?" Perry said, rubbing his hand on his round belly.

"Shall I serve dinner then?" Shayna asked, turning the volume down.

"Whats the hurry, it's only nine", Manish objected.

"Nine!" Aarav stood up from the sofa and hit his forehead with his palm while looking at the time in his cell phone, "guys I need to go", he said.

"Where?" Shayna looked surprised.

"Something urgent", he said, shaking hands with the people around.

"And you stay in touch, cutie pie", he pulled Ruby's cheek and walked towards the door. "Aarav what is this?" Shayna shouted.

"Sorry", he turned around, "I'll call you", he replied hurriedly and sprinted out.

***

"You're late", Rupali said as she opened the door.

"Very late!" Aarav nodded in apology, "Is she angry?"

"Don't know", Rupali made way for him to get in, "but she is asleep", and pointed towards Ada's room.

Blue midi, open hair, with few strands down on her cute face, black bangles and smudged eyeliner. Ada was sleeping with one palm between her cheek and pillow, with legs folded a little. The gilded pendant he gifted her on her birthday, was glinting conspicuously at her narrow throat.

He sat beside her and puffed a soft breath at her face, making those strands move slightly, "Ada" he whispered in her ear. The lids of the deep black eyes opened at his voice. "Hii", she said softly with a smile that stopped his heartbeat for a moment. He kept looking into her eyes.

"Why didn't you call me?" He said after a while. She raised herself on her haunches, "I thought you would be busy with Shayna". He touched her nose with his finger, "don't you have any rights on me?" he asked slowly. A layer of water glistened in her eyes, perhaps evincing her inability to answer his question. She moved her gaze away from his face and picked up her cell that was lying on the far corner of the bed. "It's almost ten", she said looking at the time, "shall we cook something here?" He wiped her smudged eyeliner with his thumb and showed it to her. "Wash it and put on a fresh one", he said smilingly, "I know a good restaurant in East of Kailash."

***

"Wow, this is really nice", Ada smiled as she looked around the interiors of the restaurant. Few tables and chairs, some occupied, some vacant were placed at some distance from each other, with lots of beautiful paintings hanging all around the walls, dimmed lights and slow music; a perfect place to make up for the delay.

"That corner", Aarav said pointing towards the most secluded one.

"Have you been here before?" She asked.

"Yup!"

"With Shayna?"

"No, somebody else", he smiled, as he pulled a chair for her.

"Oh! So our Casanova has one more secret, ha", she rotated her eyes.

He laughed slightly, "stupid, I came here with my brother once, at the time of admission, six years back", he said as he sat across.

"Anup bhaiya?" she smiled.

"Yes", he nodded.

"Why doesn't he come to meet you now, you have not been to Jaipur in the last year either."

"A little family problem."

"You never talk much about your family, but whatever the problem is, family is family", she said cutely. He smiled.

"So how was the party?" she raised her brows enquiringly.

"Ummm… good", he shrugged, "met some old college friends."

"Really, must have been fun, ha?"

"Ya, we were really close", he smiled and gazed around, "waiter", he called out to the nearest one.

***

"Why doesn't Rupali ever come along?" he said, sprinkling salt on his rice.

"She says, she doesn't wanna disturb us", she said with a smile. He laughed.

"Nice girl, isn't she?"

"Very helping and so-o-o cute", she nodded thoughtfully, "just glad to have a friend like her."

"Doesn't she like anyone?"

"Only her books", she bent her lips.

"And you?" he curled his mouth, with raised brows. His abrupt question made her nervous. She switched her gaze to the chicken curry, "isn't it too spicy?"

"But you like spicy food, don't you?"

"Yes", she nodded, still looking away from him.

"What's wrong, you look nervous?" He enquired. "Nothing, just studies, you know", she smiled apprehensively.

"Brilliant Ada is nervous about her studies? Ha!"

"This is the final semester", she widened her eyes.

"So?" he imitated her expression.

"So, seminar, project and then theory exams", she sighed.

"Is it all gonna be in June?" he asked while swirling his spoon in the curry.

"No, seminar and project in May and then theory papers in June."

"And what after June?" he said, trying his best to sound casual.

"Back to Goa", she answered gloomily, in a voice so painful, that it sucked the air out of his lungs. He felt dried; body and soul.

"Two butter scotch", he said to the waiter, "is that okay?" he switched his gaze towards Ada.

"Yes", she nodded slightly.

"Alright then, two butter scotch", he confirmed the desserts. "Sure sir", the waiter smiled and left.

He looked towards her. A thin smile that she portrayed was in contrast with her grieving eyes. He wanted to ask her the reason, but his mind couldn't frame that one question, which may get him the answer that his entire being was looking for. If *I can't, why don't you say something?* he thought, *perhaps you don't want to*, he inhaled a deep breath and switched his gaze to the table.

"So…" she said scratching the table cloth, "how are things at office?"

"Good", he said softly, looking towards her.

"And your new manager?" She gave a sly smile.

Her intonation brought a smile on his face, as well, "Umm… good, but she is a little too professional." The waiter came and served their order on the table, "anything else sir?" "No thank you, get the bill", Aarav replied quickly looking towards him and then returned his gaze back to her.

"That means no more fun at work?" she widened her eyes.

"Yaa… no more extra breaks at least", he frowned.

"Do one thing, set her up."

"What?" he laughed.

"Ya, give it a try", she smiled, "once she is yours, there would be no problem."

"Hah, you don't know her", he mimicked a serious note, "she is gonna eat me for dinner." She burst into laughter, enthralling his senses like always. He curled his forefinger in front of his smiling lips and let himself flow into that charming, cheering, river of laughter.

"So this is your, 'something urgent', ha?" A familiar voice brought him back. He raised his eyes. Shayna was standing in front of him, hands on her waist, eyes red with anger.

"Shayna!" he exclaimed, extremely surprised, "how come you are here?" he smiled trying to convey his words in a manner that would calm her down enough for him to have an opportunity at explaining himself. Ada turned towards her.

"He lives nearby", she pointed back, "While coming back from the party, he saw you here and called me." Aarav tilted a little to see behind her. Sam was leaning against a pillar at the end of the restaurant, chewing a gum and smiling cunningly.

"Shayna", he stood up and held her hand, "I'll explain", he said calmly. Ada was silent all the while.

"Leave me", she said loudly, making every head in the restaurant turn towards them.

"For God's sake Shayna, don't create a scene", he said scouring his gaze through the restaurant.

"What are you doing here?" She said through gritted teeth, "and who's this bitch?"

"Shayna", Aarav shouted. Ada stood up. He saw tears rolling down her eyes, as she walked away.

"Ada", he tried to follow her, but Shayna held his hand, "if you go after her, you'll lose me."

"Go to hell", he snapped at her looking straight into her eyes and jerked his hand off her grip. He took out his wallet and plonked a couple of thousand rupee notes on the table and walked out of the restaurant.

***

As he couldn't see her at the end of the lane, he took out his cell and dialed her number.

"Ada, where are you?" He said as she received the call, after around half a dozen rings.

"I'm in an auto", she replied.

"I'm sorry."

"No, that's okay", she sounded a little choked, "I should have realized, you are somebody's boyfriend."

"You know I don't love her", he said firmly, "and you are", he paused for a second, "my best friend", he said. Only he knew how hard he had gulped down the words he actually wanted to say.

"You too are my best friend Aarav", she said softly, "but it's better I leave now, I'll call you later."

"Ada please don't go like this."

She almost broke down, "bye Aarav." He could hear her choking right before she hung up.

He felt something within himself, shivering like hell. He kept looking at the display, till the clotting tears in his eyes blurred its image.

"Aarav", he heard Shayna's softened voice, from right behind.

"Aa…Aarav", she kept her hand on his shoulder. He turned around to face her. She hugged him and started crying. He didn't say a word. He did not feel her hug. He felt nothing.

***

THREE MONTHS LATER

Not even the cheering crowd of around thousand employees, gathered in a farm house in the outskirts of Gurgaon for the company's annual function, could lighten up his mood. As against his presumption, the party seemed boring, or perhaps it was his own feelings, getting reflected to make things meaningless and gloomy for him.

The racking restlessness he was gripped with for the last three months, didn't seem to loosen. Movies, beer, parties, no matter what he tried, what he did, it just couldn't get her out of his mind. *Perhaps this was supposed to happen,* he kept saying to himself over and over again. It was the only sentence that repressed his suffering, for a moment or two. But at the same time, he kept wondering, had the things been same, if only it could have happened the way it was supposed to be, on a happy note, with proper goodbyes. *Perhaps it wouldn't have caused this kind of awkwardness in my life*, was the answer of his mind every time. But the sheer vacuity her absence created in his heart, never actually did agree with his mind.

Standing at the most secluded end, lost in his own thoughts, he saw Mr. Rickey, the charismatic managing director of the company, walking up the stage. Being a big fan of him, he couldn't resist taking a few steps towards the stage to listen to him. "I know we are here for a party and not sessions", bringing a smile on every face, he started, "as we all know the annual turn over of the company for the financial year 2012, was 370 million dollars", he said with a proud emphasis on the dollar amount, and the environment filled with applauses, "but..but", he waved his hands to calm them down, "the year 2013 hasn't been good so far, in the months of April and May, we were not able to get even close to the projected figure", he stopped for a while, "but I'm sure we will be able to make up for it in June by attaining 36 million", he said raising his own brows, perhaps at the hulk projection and surveyed the crowd, "will we?" he shouted piercing the silence. "Yes!!!" The crowd roared with enthusiasm, straining every ear, but bringing peace on Mr. Rickey's face, "alright then enjoy the party", he said and a loud rock music followed.

A general guess says that everybody might have been thinking about the projected amount but Aarav was one person thinking about the month, 'June'. *This would be her last month in Delhi*, he thought, though he tried his best not to; but words, coupled into a discomforting sentence had already thrust into his mind. He looked around, to be sure that nobody saw him with that dismal expression. He knew that his face right now would be an open book to those who look at it. His inner being was not equipped to hold back his turmoil as well as put up a façade acceptable to others. He relaxed on seeing everybody, either busy at a food counter or dancing in the artificial rain, arranged at the other end of the lawn. He let out a quick sigh and moved to the bar, to get himself a drink.

"Hii Aarav," a sweet voice hit his ears from behind as he placed the order for his drink. He turned around and saw Meenakshi, his first line manager, standing in front of him with a warm smile on her face.

"How are you?" She said in her usual professional tone.

"Good", Aarav smiled back.

"Where's Neil? Haven't seen him around."

"Don't know", he shrugged slightly, "he didn't call me."

"Nor has he called me, if you get to speak to him, ask him to give me a call", she said and moved ahead to the other end of the bar.

Her enquiry made him realize, how deeply he had been implicated in his thoughts, that he missed the absence of his only friend. He felt a little guilty for his so-lost behavior. Picking up the drink the bartender just made for him, he walked towards the quiet end of the farm house to call him.

"Hey hunter, where are you?" He enquired as Neil received the call.

"I'm home", Neil said in a frail voice.

"Why aren't you here at the function?"

"Are you there?" Aarav asked again when there was no reply.

"Ya, just a little headache." Neil responded with the same frail voice.

"Don't you lie to me."

"Aarav", Neil said, his voice completely shattered, "can you come to my place after the party is over?"

The way he put his request, it took Aarav no time to gauge his miserable mood, and a part of his mind sensed the reason as well. "I'll be there in an hour", he assured him and disconnected the call.

***

Red sunken eyes, unshaved pale face, disheveled hair and lots of empty bottles of beer, were enough hints for Aarav to understand that the situation was far worse than he had expected. The way Neil was trying to avoid eye contact with him, the way he was failing to put his breathing in order and the way his hands were trembling, he realized that something was terribly wrong.

Aarav got down from the sofa and sat beside him on the floor, "what happened?" He asked in a soft tone, putting the half finished bottle of beer aside. Neil turned towards him, cold red eyes, all wet.

"Sakshi is getting married next month", he said after a while. The tremulous pain in his voice sent a shiver down Aarav's spine.

"What?" He exclaimed.

Neil swallowed hard, "Ya to a computer engineer settled in the UK."

"Suddenly?" Aarav frowned, "I mean I spoke to you two days ago and I believe everything was okay up until then, wasn't it?"

"She called me yesterday."

"Is she okay?" Aarav said softly.

"Ya", Neil's face had a thin sarcastic smile hanging on a side, "she sounded perfectly okay."

"What do you mean?" A surprised Aarav stared at him for a second, "she wants to marry you, doesn't she?"

"No", Neil's tone was cynical, "she wanted to, but now she has a better option."

"Are you crazy?" He yelled in disbelief.

Neil looked at him, the pain in his eyes was taken over by an angry color, "not after this", he said without expression, stretching his hand to pick up the half finished beer bottle. "She asked me to forget everything", he drank a good amount in a go, "everything", he repeated;

more to himself than to Aarav, plonking the bottle beside him, "you know what? This is how some people are, option friendly, the richer the better."

The silence thereafter made every word spoken by Neil echo in his mind so loudly that it started aching wearily, as if a subconscious part of him was agreeing with it, making him suddenly realize that he already knew this sullied reality.

"Wanna have tea?" Aarav said pressing his thumb against his temple.

"Ya", Neil heaped himself up from the floor, "let's go out", he said.

***

"Here, take it." Aarav passed him a cup of tea while making himself comfortable on a smirched bench of the tea stall at the end of Neil's lane and lit up the cigarette in his hand.

"Which one is that?" Neil grimaced while pulling a chair for himself, "don't they have Marlboro?"

"No", Aarav smiled, "only Gold Flake", and passed it to him.

"Aah! It's so strong", Neil cried as he took a puff. Aarav was still smiling, but at the back of his mind, Neil's words were hitting hard. "What you said back in the room, you really think that's always true?" He said, looking into his tea cup.

Neil turned his face towards him, "the richer the better?"

"Yes", Aarav nodded.

"Of course, see what Sakshi did to me", he stopped for a moment, "one day Shayna might do the same thing."

Aarav looked into his eyes, "I don't think she will", he said.

"You really sure of her love?"

"No, but I'm sure she won't be able to find an option better than me", he twisted the corner of his lips, "you ever heard of Khanna Developers?"

"Ya, read about their multi crore projects on the Delhi - Jaipur highway a few times", he frowned, "why?"

"That's my dad's", Aarav said even before Neil had finished his question, leaving him dumbfound, with his mouth open. "So you're a millionaire?" he said after a while. Aarav shrugged innocently.

"Why do you work then?" He threw his hands in the air. "I mean, you can live in a lavish house and ride a BMW."

Aarav smiled, "that's exactly what I used to do up until two years ago", he said, "but my father's speeches and taunts, that I'm good for nothing after I left my first job at The J's, made me take this decision to stand on my own two feet", he stopped, "but Shayna knows about this and what you said today is giving me a feeling that all she is interested in is my money."

Neil kept his tea cup beside and turned towards him, "so you think Shayna is with you only in the hope that one day you will inherit your millions?"

"Seems so", he shrugged, "she keeps talking about opening a business, perhaps she wants me to use my dad's money."

Neil went thoughtful for a moment, but returned with a spark in his eyes, "you know what? We can get this cleared now."

"How?"

"Text her that the entire business has been ramped down", Neil said at once. Aarav gave him a confused look. "Look", he continued, "your Khanna Developers is no Kingfisher that it's bankruptcy is supposed to become a national news, so it will take her some time before she finds out the truth", he stopped and looked straight into Aarav's eyes, "and trust me, that time will be good enough to get things clear."

"You really think it's a good idea?"

"Of course it is", he said.

Aarav took a deep breath, "Alright but then you do it", he said and handed him his phone.

Neil gave him a disapproving look, but obliged after a while. He took the cell phone from Aarav's hand and started fidgeting with it. "What exactly are you gonna write?" Aarav asked.

"This", Neil said, "Curt and effective", he smiled and showed him the display which said, "Business all rampd down, dad fell sick after filing for bankruptcy, going home for a few days."

Neil jerked his brows, "shall I?" he said with his finger close to the send option on the screen. Aarav twisted his mouth in confusion and then raised his shoulder, inhaling a deep breath, "okay", he said, letting a huge sigh out.

Neil stared at him for a few seconds for confirmation and clicked on 'send'.

***

It was the third cup of tea they were silently relishing and yet seemed to be ready for a few more. The vision of passing vehicles on the main road in front, the evening wind and hot tea were working out well, while they were waking up to reality.

"Why did you leave the party midway? I asked you to come after it's over", Neil said breaking the long silence.

Aarav made a face, "it was too boring "and do you know what they are targeting for June?" Neil shrugged in ignorance. "36 million", Aarav completed in frustration.

"Really?"

"Yup." Aarav smiled lazily.

"There is no seasonality", he said, "June is gonna be a tough month."

"Ya really tough, at least for me", Aarav said thoughtfully, as if the words just slipped out his mouth, but somewhere within himself, he knew that he actually wanted them to.

"Why especially for you?" Neil frowned.

Aarav turned his face towards him, the gripping tension causing a visible tautness in his jaw muscles, "she would go back to Goa by the month end", he said slowly.

"You still think about her?"

"A lot actually", he sighed, "though I have been trying not to, but just can't help it."

"Well, that's love I guess", Neil smiled.

"No", he smiled back, "I think it's the unexpected way we parted."

"Did you two speak after the restaurant incident?"

"Seldom, that too when I called her", he shook his head, with his lips bent down in a frown, "she says she doesn't wanna disturb my love life."

"Hah", Neil laughed, "half an hour and your love hasn't replied yet", he said showing him his cell.

Aarav smiled, "*Sutta*?" He stood up.

"Ya, but not Gold Flake", Neil made a face, "maybe we can get Marlboro there", he said pointing towards a shop across the main road.

"I'll get one", Aarav said and walked towards the shop.

"Get five", he heard Neil's voice when he was in the middle of the road. He turned around and saw him with a stretched palm, showing all the fingers and suddenly Neil diverted his gaze and shouted, "Aarav." His voice coupled with the sound of a skidding vehicle reached his ears, only a fraction of second before his reflexes could make him look in the direction Neil was looking at, a speeding car hit him. He felt a strong jerk and rolled down the road, until his head struck the divider. Blood was dripping down his face and neck, soaking him in its warmth. Everything around started getting darker. He saw Neil and several other people running towards him. "Aarav, Aarav", Neil's nervous voice was hitting his eardrum from his right. "Don't call my family", Aarav said wearily, before he closed his eyes.

***

"Hey man, how are you?" Neil said as Aarav opened his eyes. He found himself in the middle of a room with white curtains, shining floor and some medicines on a small table beside the bed, certain it was a hospital room.

"You have been unconscious for the last twenty four hours, thank God you opened your eyes", Neil said pressing his hands slightly, "she is downstairs for some paperwork, let me call her to get the doctor along".

"Who?" Aarav winced in pain.

"Ada."

The name itself brought an instinctive aliveness in Aarav's faded nerves. A wave of incomprehensible happiness travelled through his whole body at the mere mention of her presence around. "How come is she here?" He asked, being unable to stop the lips from curling into a big smile, despite the increasing pain in the wounds on his forehead and neck on stretching the facial muscles.

Neil turned towards him, "I called her", he said and showed him his HTC. "You remember this was with me", he twisted his mouth thoughtfully, "actually I got nervous, handling the situation alone, so I called Shayna first, but she said she was busy and will call back", he stopped for a moment, "perhaps she doesn't give a damn to bankrupt people", he smiled, "so I called Ada, and she has been here since last evening", he said and walked towards the door. He opened it, stopped for a second and then turned around, "she really cares for you, I saw her crying in the lobby outside, a couple of times", he said and walked out.

Aarav looked at the ceiling with a broad smile on his face. He could feel the increase in the warmth and pressure of blood, all through his veins, perhaps at the inciting thought of seeing her in a short while. His heart was pounding hard, to mark its own excitement. Suddenly, a sound of footstep close to the door made him turn his face towards it and his smile stretched to its limit as if some instincts sensed who it could be. The door opened sending a warm shaft of delight down his spine. In slippers, Capri and t-shirt, Ada entered with wet eyes and a big smile on her face.

She walked upto his bed and took his hand in hers, "can't you even cross a road properly?" She complained, half smiling, half crying. Pain from all over his body, seemed being drained out at her soothing touch. He curled his fingers into a fist and touched her nose, "how are you?" He asked weakly. Tears rolled down her eyes, "I missed you", she replied.

***

"There's nothing to worry about, you will be fine in about three weeks", the doctor said, smiling at Aarav, "it was just loss of blood and a broken ankle", he added a little later, looking towards Neil and Ada, who stood beside anxiously, while the doctor was checking his vitals.

"Doctor, is there any other formality or paper work that's left?" Neil asked.

"No", he smiled again, "his health insurance and employer will take it from here", he said and left the room with his team.

"Thanks", Aarav said, as Neil and Ada shifted their gaze from the closing door to him.

"Say thanks to Midllan", Neil said, "you know I informed Meenakshi and she was here in an hour and got all the finances approved by the company", he stopped for a while and twisted his lips sadly, "but being a bitch, as you already know; she asked me to come to office today, at least for an hour", he sighed, "so I gotta go."

"You must be tired as well, go back home", Aarav said to Ada.

"No, I'll stay", she said firmly.

"You two really need some time together", Neil said with a sly smile on his face and walked out of the room.

It was just the two of them in the room, "So", Ada said, pulling a chair for herself.

"So?" he smiled.

"Umm... how's your ankle?"

"It hurts, but not as much as the heart did when you left that day", he laughed, "quite a drama queen, aren't you?"

"No yaar, I'm your friend, why would I want to be the reason for your messed up love life."

He kept looking into her dark eyes, peeping from behind a few strands of hair fallen down on her face, "Shayna and I are no longer together", he said after a while, expecting to see a streak of happiness in those eyes, but on the contrary it's colour changed into a grieving one, "why?" She almost yelled. The word felt like a physical blow to him, or perhaps it was her unexpected reaction that sent a wave of strange disappointment through his body. *Perhaps you don't feel a thing, all I'm for you is just a friend*, he didn't understand why that thought struck his mind, although he himself never admitted to her that she is more than just a friend.

"Tell me, why?" She asked again.

"Nothing, just like that", he nodded.

'Was it because of me?" she said slowly, biting her lower lip.

"No", he laughed at her cute gesture, "when are your exams gonna start?"

"Next week", she said, the melancholic expression still intact.

"Well you should be stu…", before he could complete, the door swung open and a nurse entered. "Medicine time", she said as she reached the table beside him and gave him a few capsules and a bitter syrup, "sleep well", she said with a smile and walked out.

"God! It tastes like hell", Aarav made a face. She smiled adoringly.

"Ya, I was saying that you should be studying then."

"That's okay", she shrugged, "I'm kind of prepared". He smiled, "How are Jenny aunty and Peter uncle?"

"Good", she smiled.

"And Rupali?" He said throwing his brows up, foxily.

"Ya she is fine", she stretched her smile, "you know what? She came here with me yesterday, went back around ten."

"And you chose to stay?"

"Of course I had to", she said, "you won't believe, but I was missing you very badly yesterday", she went thoughtful for a moment and then smiled again, "perhaps, because Rupali brought fish from the market, you remember last time I cooked it for you, you didn't like it much, but I have learnt an all new way…", she kept on talking as usual and he listened to her, missing terribly the comprehension part, as he felt drowsy, perhaps under the influence of those medicines. But he kept listening to her, for long, with a thin smile continuously lingering on his face, till sleep completely took over his senses.

***

The bright sunlight, through the glass window, made him open his eyes and he found her sleeping on the chair with her head down on his bed, so close to his hand that he could feel her warm breath on it. He felt a little guilty for being the reason of her trouble, but didn't wake her up, with the intent of not disturbing the sweet dream she seemed to be in, as the corner of her lips were curled into a mesmerizingly beautiful soft smile, just adding to her divine cuteness.

Her eyes, though closed, were so gravitational, that he couldn't take his own off them, and to his surprise, he found her stirring as if she could sense his gaze on her, even in her sleep. Her slight movements let a strand of hair loose from behind her ear and fall on her face, causing those dark eyelashes, to flicker. His hand, without waiting for a signal from his mind, quickly reached out to her face and with the softest possible touch, curled the strand to tuck it back from where it fell. He tried to pull his hand back but becoming a complete rebel, it chose to linger around. His fingers, so close to her face, trembled slightly with the intoxicating desire of touching her. She stirred again and his fingers, quickly curled back into the palm, as if, it got an electric shock. He smiled. The door swung opened and a nurse entered, "good morning" she said a little loudly. "Shhhh!" he hushed, "she is slee…", he stopped for a moment, as he saw her waking up, "…was sleeping", completed slowly, letting his shoulders hang down.

"Good morning", Ada smiled sluggishly, wiping her eye with her palm.

"Morning", Aaarv smiled at her, "you had a better place to sleep", he said pointing towards the velvet couch near the window.

"I just fell asleep", she made a face. Aarav and the nurse both smiled at her gesture.

"You better go back home and have some good sleep", he said caressing her head, while the nurse kept a capsule in his other hand.

"But how can I leave you like this?"

He smiled, "I'm fine", he said, "and they are taking good care of me", he added, looking towards the nurse, who smiled back and stamped another capsule in his hand. He made a face.

"Okay, but I'll come back in the evening", she said looking into his eyes.

"Ada, you have your exams starting next week." She kept looking at him wantingly, her eyes completely dissident of the suggestion he was trying to make. He twisted his mouth in submission, "Okay, but just for an hour or two", he said.

"Two or three", she replied almost immediately, making his lips stretch into a smile and then into laughter.

***

The setting sun was increasing his impatience, he had a hard time controlling after the long day. Leaning against the backrest of the bed, he was wavering, with his cell in his hand, thinking whether or not to text her. *I must*, he said to himself, after letting a huge breath out. He stayed still for a moment and then started swaying again, thinking what to text her. *Where are you?*He nodded. *Naa, it would be stupid to ask her that, I mean I was the one suggesting her not to come*, he said to himself, *umm… what's up? Naa*, he shook his head again, making a sound, pressing his tongue against his palate, in rejection of his second thought, *this will sound even more stupid*, he curled his lips down. Suddenly his phone vibrated and the bent down lips spread out into a big smile, on seeing the display. It was a message from Ada. He quickly opened it. It said, 'jst tuk an auto.. wl be thr in 30 mins'. He twisted his mouth in surprise, smile still intact, *seems like you can still get into my mind*, he said slowly, looking into the cell.

After what felt like thirty years, the clock on the wall finally struck six; thirty minutes after her message. He checked the message again to reconfirm the time he received it. Being unable to wait any longer, he typed 'Whr hv u rchd?' and sent it. 'At ur door☺', came her instant reply. And a second later, she walked in; designer skirt, light pink top, matching ear rings and open hair, she looked like an angel straight out of a magical fairy tale book. "Hiiii!" she said, with a big smile on her face. "Hii", he replied slowly, being completely lost in her breathtaking beauty.

"Is it really you, Ada?" he said, touching her hand with his finger.

She laughed as she sat on the chair, "just felt like doing this, after a long time", she said, raising her shoulders. He smiled, "what have you got in such a big purse?" he said.

"This?" She took out a small bouquet and some chocolates.

"You never forget to do these stupid things, do you?"

"What's stupid about them?" she said, keeping the flowers on the side table, "they will get you well soon", she smiled, "and these chocolates are for me", she added cuddling them close to her heart, in her usual childish countenance, "but I can share them with you", she laughed.

This smile he sighed, *I missed it so much*, he thought. "So how was your day?"

"Good", she said, "I slept, ate yummy Maggi for lunch and watched my Shahrukh's RNBDJ"

"Surinder Sahni?" he laughed, "nice movie isn't it?"

"Amazing!"

"Hah! Now you are being a typical Shahrukh's fan."

"No really, it is, every time I watch it, I laugh and I cry."

He smiled, "is there a movie which doesn't make you cry?"

"Of course there are, do you think I cry every day watching television?"

"Television?" He was surprised, "you guys have bought one?"

"No-o-o, at Singh aunty's house", she smirked, "where do you think I watched RNBDJ?"

"Yaa," he gave her a now-I-remember look. "So, how are they and does Singh uncle still say, rent on time", he mimicked his voice. She burst into laughter, the crackling laughter he was listening to after such a long time, the laughter that he missed so badly, the laughter that could draw every single chord of his heart into some magical melody.

It wasn't until his phone vibrated on receiving a message, that he realized that they were talking for the last three hours. He smiled, 'time just flies with her', he thought. "It's Neil's message", he said, "the entire team is gonna pay me a visit tomorrow."

"Your company is really nice, and the employees there are even more so", she said.

"Not just nice, it's a great place to work", he said with a hint of pride in his eyes. He looked at the wall clock a second later and added, "well madam, it's already nine, I think you should leave". She twisted her face, twisting her lips sideways.

"I don't want you to take auto or taxi too late at night."

She nodded,"but it's not too late yet."

He smiled, "okay, but then just ten more minutes", he said.

"Twenty please", she said tilting her head in one direction. He kept looking at her innocent eyes, making him fall short of any possible word in refusal, "okay", he said, with a broad smile on his face.

***

With his head leaning against the backrest of the bed, he kept flipping the pages of the not so interesting magazine, which he had been trying to read for almost the entire week. His days in hospital were passing a little faster than he expected them to and he knew his heart wasn't too happy with it, perhaps because he knew these were the only days he would be able to meet her. Although sitting all day long, going through magazines or sleeping, was a little too boring, but the only thing that was keeping him sane; infact excited, was her expected visit.

"Hey Rocco", Neil smiled as he entered his room.

And sometimes these unexpected ones as well.

Aarav raised himself a little higher against the backrest, "Neil", he smiled, keeping the magazine back on the table, "how come you're here so early in the morning today?" He said, looking at the wall clock, which struck eleven.

"Aah just completed the fucking sunrise shift", he said as he pulled himself a chair.

"Ya, you look fucked", Aarav laughed.

Neil made a face, "saale, you've been resting in this lavish room, at the expense of the dollars we are collecting". The room reverberated with Aarav's laughter, "get your ankle broken and you can be here as well."

Neil smiled, "how long is that gonna take?" He gestured towards his plastered feet.

"Just a few more days."

"Get well soon man, it's been a long time since we have boozed togeth…" his voice slipped into silence for a moment as his gaze fell on the bouquet, on the table, "who got you this?", he said.

A gentle smile floated across Aarav's face, "Ada", he replied slowly.

"Does she come here?"

"Of course", Aarav laughed faintly, "how do think she got me this, by courier?"

"I mean, does she come here often or just … "

"Everyday", Aarav said, before letting him complete.

"She likes you a lot", Neil's lips stretched into a mild smile, "don't you think it could be love?"

Aarav shrugged, with his lips curled down, "I don't think so, she never says anything"

"And what about you?" Neil shot another question, for which Aarav, by any means, had no answer. He kept looking into Neil's eyes, "tea?" he said after a few seconds.

***

"And you know what, there are people who take even worse calls", Aarav laughed, "You remember Ronit? Once he said, that too to a lady, 'madam you give me five hundred dollars and I'll give you one shot'" Neil almost dropped the tea on himself, as he burst into a sudden laughter at his intonation. "Man, you almost copied his voice", Neil was still laughing.

The clock struck twelve and Aarav noticed Neil wiping his face and stretching his jaded eyes to keep himself awake. "I think you should go get some sleep", he said.

"Yaa, I will", Neil replied slowly, "that's the only thing left for the day."

"Your eyes are all red."

"They are like this all the time these days", he said in a low, melancholic voice. Aarav knew exactly what he meant, "did you speak to Sakshi?" He said. Neil shook his head.

Aarav kept looking at the changes in the expression of his face from smiling to angry to grieving, "I think you should, at least once."

"She left me", his voice trembled, "why should I call her?" Aarav remained silent for sometime, "got a *sutta*?" He said, jerking his brows up, with a sheepish smile on his face.

Neil smiled with him, "ya, I do, but where will we smoke?" He frowned slightly.

Aarav winked, pointing towards the left end of the room, "in the bathroom."

"Behanchoo."

"No, I'm serious", Aarav got down from the bed and balanced himself slowly, on the floor, "let's go", he said.

"You landed in this hospital, because of this", Neil said as he passed him the cigarette after taking a puff.

"Hah! What ever happens, happens for good", Aarav smiled.

"You mean Shayna?"

Aarav nodded as he passed him the cigarette back, for the last possible puff.

"What a bitch!" Neil snapped.

***

It was his ninth morning in the hospital and just like the last eight, a pleasant smile stretched across his face, even before he opened his eyes. The reason being her morning messages in his phone, waiting to be read. With his heart tickling softly, his hand crawled under the pillow and pulled his cell out. The smile turned into a huge grin as he opened the message, 'Good morning☺. wl rply aftr papr', but the grin disappeared as he read it. "God! It's her exam today, and you forgot to wish her luck last night", he said to himself, *you're such a jerk.* 'Mrnin. u mst b in the examntn room..bt stl..ol the best☺!! An u cud hav reminded me while chatng last nit', he typed the reply and sent it, while his face stayed twisted in regret.

After trying to read magazines, playing video games in his cell and solving the tiring crossword puzzles in the newspaper all morning, he was almost through with waiting for the clock to strike one. The century long two hours and thirty minutes had passed, but the last fifteen minutes were just not dying. The hour hand was almost there, but the minute hand was still crawling like a lazy snail, getting on his nerves. 'I should text her to call back once she is out of the examination room', he thought and sent her a message asking for a call back. And surprising him, like always, she called him in the next couple of seconds. "Hey!" he said, "you got out?"

"Ya, a few minutes ago", she said.

"Then why didn't you call me?"

"I thought you must be asleep after taking your afternoon dose of medicines."

He sighed, "don't you think you are way too modest?" She laughed.

"No really, I'm serious. You can't tell me about your exam a day before, thinking I might be bothered by wishing you luck. You can't call me, thinking I might be asleep and, an ... ", he stumbled, but added slowly, "you didn't contact me for three months, thinking that might turn my love life upside down.", he let a deep sigh out, "well you must be the greatest person alive", he said with bare sarcasm.

"Alright, I'm sorry ", she said cutely, "can I meet you now?"

"For what?" he still sounded angry.

"Nothing, just wanted to bother you." He tried not to, but burst into laughter.

***

The lazy hours after lunch had always been difficult for him to pass, and the ones in hospital could have been impossible, with practically nothing to do. But luckily, he had a lot to think about. Resting the back of his palm against his forehead, he stared at the ceiling, being completely lost in the recollection of her cute blabs. Her stupid words, her childish expressions, kept stalking his mind, making his lips spread into soft smiles every two seconds. *When you're not around, all I think about is you, your talks, and your smiles; like it adds a meaning to every beat of my heart. I wait all day for the beautiful evening that brings you here and I just don't know why!*, he tossed himself on the bed and looked out of the window. Two sparrows playing with each other deepened the smile on his face, *you're really something, Ada*, he said slowly and closed his eyes, but only for a moment, as a sudden desire of hearing her voice made him open his eyes and he stretched his hand to pick his cell up from the table.

She must be studying, he thought scratching his forehead with his thumb. *So what?* said another voice in his head. *She is already spending so much time here,* countered the first voice. He sighed, *but just a few minutes is not gonna make any difference,* one of the Aaravs won and he dialed her number.

"Hii", she replied almost immediately, "was thinking about you only", she chirped in her usual tone.

His heart floated in some fairy clouds at her voice and a big smile sprouted on his face, "really?" He said in a rather blase voice, not willing to let her guess his stupid excitement at her voice.

"Yup, was planning to cook something for you."

"Don't tell me it's Maggi or macroni."

She laughed, "it is macroni."

"God! For the last three weeks you are getting me these junks."

"No, this one will be different, I learnt it on television, I'm sure you'll like it."

"Ada", he said in a serious cadence, "stop experimenting on me." He heard her laughing again.

"Are you really serious?"

"Of course, I am."

"Okay", she said slowly, "but this is all I can cook apart from fried fish."

This time it was his turn to laugh, "just kidding", he said, "get me whatever you've cooked."

"*Saale kutte*, you scared me."

"What time are you gonna be here?" He said still laughing.

"In about two hours", she said.

"Alright, see you then", he replied. "Bye."

"Bye." He disconnected the call but kept looking into the cell with a huge grin on his face, till his mind or perhaps the medicines caught him up for the afternoon nap.

***

"Now try and walk, putting as less pressure as you can on this leg", the doctor said, as he made Aarav walk just after taking the plaster off, "and yet keep it straight and flat on the floor", he added.

Aarav took a few steps and realized that it was easier to do so with plaster on, "doctor it's hurting", he said twisting his face in pain.

"It will", the doctor smiled, "for the next few days, but very soon it will be fine."

"So you mean to say, I have to stay here for a few more days."

"Yes, two, we will discharge you on the twenty second", he kept his hand on Aarav's shoulder and smiled again, "so just show as much improvement as you can in the next two days", he encouraged him and walked out of the room.

After completing his second round in the room, he sat on the bed with his legs hanging down and his hand slipping under his pillow to take his cell out. *I must tell her this*, he thought and typed a message, 'doctr sd wl dschrg me on 22nd', and sent it.

It wasn't even ten seconds that his phone vibrated on receiving her reply. 'Wow!! Congo..party thn..an u knw wat that's the last day of my exam☺', it said. He smiled mildly but his heart twisted on seeing her 'wow', *perhaps she is so happy about going back to Goa*. Feeling a little low, he typed his reply, "sure!! lets go out fr dinnr the same day.. and u've booked ur tickt fr 23rd.. rit?". As he sent it, he switched his gaze from his cell to the glass window in front and felt his heart cramping at the fear of getting another 'wow', or smiley. He couldn't understand the reason, but somewhere deep down, he wanted her to be sad just like he was, but unfortunately he just couldn't stand her being sad either. His phone vibrated again and he opened the message, "Grt idea☺..I'll come there aftr the exam..k ..an ya fr 23rd", it said.

That one smiley sunk his heart. He laughed faintly, perhaps at himself and kept the phone back under the pillow. He walked upto the window and stood there, frozen, looking out till the retrenching sunlight completely vanished from the horizon.

***

Just as he came out of the shower, he saw the display of his phone, kept on the bed, blinking and it's strong vibration was loud and clear in the silent room. Despite the hurting leg, he took quick steps towards the bed and picked it up. It was Neil calling. A thin screen of disappointment veiled his heart, perhaps because he was expecting Ada's call. *She must not have got out of the examination room yet*, consoling himself, he received the call, "Hey bud", he said smilingly.

"You're up", Neil said excitedly.

"Ya, and I got the jeans and shirt you left for me here", he said looking into a carry bag on the table, "why didn't you wake me up, when you came here?"

"Hah, you were sleeping like an ass", Neil laughed, "And that's my favorite black shirt, so you better take good care of it."

Aarav laughed slightly, "ya sure."

"So ready to get back to work", Neil said.

"Yaa…", Aarav stretched the word thoughtfully, "may be from the coming Monday."

"And what time are you gonna get out of there."

"Umm… just waiting for Ada, she said she will be here after completing her exam."

"Seems like somebody has got this evening planned", Neil laughed teasingly.

Aarav smiled, completely unaware of the hint of shyness in it, "just taking her out for dinner tonight", he stopped and let out a brief sigh, "she is going back tomorrow", he said slowly.

"Are you okay?"

"Ya", Aarav smiled, "perfectly okay", he said with all the fake confidence.

"Alright, and I'll come down to your place tomorrow evening", Neil said.

"Is it your off?"

"No, I'm gonna take a leave."

"Well that sounds good", Aarav bent his lips down.

"And listen don't forget to take numbers of a few sexy nurses, before you leave", Neil said and they both burst out into laughter.

"See you tomorrow", Aarav said, still laughing, but his uneasiness was clearly discernible in his eyes.

***

"All set?" sitting on the couch, playing video game in his cell, Aarav heard a male voice at the door. He raised his eyes and saw his doctor standing, with a smiling face. "Yes doc", he smiled back and stood up.

"Keep doing the exercises and come down here every two weeks for routine checkups", doctor said while giving him a firm handshake.

"Sure."

"And just don't forget to take your medicines."

"Ah! They are really a lot in numbers, I often get confused", he smiled.

"But I don't", Ada entered the room with a huge grin on her face. Aarav's thin smile turned into a big one at her sight. "Hii doctor", she said, "I'll explain this to him", she added while taking the prescription in her hand. "These two before breakfast, this one in the afternoon before lunch, this one before and this syrup after dinner", she said scrolling her finger down the prescription.

"Yes", the doctor said, "that's right." She smiled.

"All the best", the doctor said and walked out.

"So how was your exam?" Aarav said in a low dull voice.

"Good", she said rather loudly, in contrast with his tone, or so he felt, and took out a chocolate from her purse, "this is for you", she smiled.

"For what?"

"For getting well", she said and pressed the chocolate in his hand. He smiled faintly, "let's go", he said.

"Sure", she chirped while holding his arm.

"Yaar I can walk by myself", he almost shouted at her. "I'm sorry", she said slowly and took her hand off his arm. He felt guilty for his rude behavior but little did he understand the reason behind it. 'God! Why am I shouting at her', he looked at her face, as innocent as her eyes. He took a deep breath and swung his eyes from her towards the floor and then his gaze fell on the dairymilk in his hand that she just gave him. A mild smile spread on his face, "You remember", he said slowly, turning his face back towards her, "you used to give me this every time you had to see a new place."

She smiled, "that was a part of our deal."

"Deal!" he laughed out loud, and slowly the laughter trailed off into a gentle smile, "I was your guide that time", he seemed a little lost in his memories.

"And you were pretty good."

He looked into her eyes, "good?" he widened his own, "the best", he said a second later, "is there a place in Delhi I didn't take you to?"

She started thinking, tapping her lips with her forefinger, while they entered the lift. "Zoo", she said, as the doors closed. Aarav laughed, "that's for children". She made a face, looking at him, still thoughtful, "And India gate!!" She almost yelled, a second later.

"Are you serious?" he frowned, "you've never been to India gate?" She shook her head like a child, "you never took me there."

"Well, I always assumed that you have been there", he shrugged, "it's a beautiful place to spend evenings."

"Then lets go there", she said as the lift stopped at the ground floor.

"Now?"

"Yaa", she jerked her shoulders up in excitement, "it's evening." He kept looking at her, "and dinner?" he said slowly, "I planned to take you to…"

"Forget your plan", she interrupted, "we are going to India gate", she said with a huge grin on her face.

***

Sparkling in the dazzling lights, against the dark evening, like a drop of dew gleaming on a black rose petal, India Gate looked incredibly beautiful. Standing at the end of the road in front of the Gate, they completely lost themselves in the drawing glare of the magnificent structure.

"Wow!" she said softly, after a while and clung to his arm. Her warm touch amidst the cold evening wind took a few beats off his heart. He looked at her face glowing in the faded, yellow street lights and a strange wish thrust in his heart. *May this moment freeze, may you and I stay here, like this, forever.* She turned her face towards him, as if she heard him. He swung his gaze off her, in an attempt to pull himself together, "I...I told you, it's beautiful", he shrugged, pointing towards the Gate. She kept looking at him, with her dark big eyes, wide opened, "yes it is", she said after a few seconds.

After taking a close view of the monument, they looked around for a quiet place to sit. "There!" She yelled, pointing towards a vacant metal bench under a Gulmohar tree. Aarav smiled at her childish intonation, "come", he said a second later.

"I didn't know this place was so beautiful", she said as they sat on the bench, "you should have shown me this earlier."

He just smiled. *I have been here so many times, but it never appeared as beautiful as it does today, with you,* he thought.

"What?" She asked. He shook his head, still smiling, "nothing", he said after a brief pause.

She kept looking at him for a while and then turned her eyes away. "Hey!" she shouted all of a sudden, "is that pani puri?"

Aarav hit his forehead with his palm and then turned towards her, "yes." She laughed, "lets go", she said and dragged him along.

"You had more than ten, I guess", he said as they came back to the bench. She kept her hand bag on the bench and looked at him with a winning smile on her face, "sixteen!" she said proudly as she sat down.

He widened his eyes at her answer, "really!" he exclaimed slowly, while making himself comfortable beside her, "If you keep hogging on these junks, you will soon be an elephant."

She laughed, "No I won't."

"How can you be so sure?"

"Don't know", she shrugged, "But I will never get fat."

He smiled, "ten, twenty years from now, you will be like her", he said pointing towards a fat lady, across the garden. She looked at her and then turned her face back to him, "not even in twenty five years", she said confidently, "you may get old and shattered, the way you smoke."

He laughed, "How will we get to know?"

"Yaa… you are right", she said gently, thought for a while, and then looked back into his eyes. "you know what, there is a way", she said with beaming eyes.

"And what is that?" he pried.

"Let's meet here after twenty five years."

"What!" he let out a disbelieving chuckle.

"Yaa", she said rather seriously, "June 22, 2038, same time", she checked her phone for a second, "08:30 a.m.", she said looking into his eyes.

"You can't be serious", he said, lips still curved into a smile, which gradually disappeared at the sight of confidence in her eyes, "are you?" he frowned.

"Yes I am."

"Twenty five years?" He curled his lips down, looking into the darkness, "perhaps you won't even remember my name", he turned towards her, "but still I will come", he said, looking straight in her eyes, "and you?"

"No matter what", she said firmly.

The deepening darkness was adding to the calmness. But they were still seated on that bench, as if they had became a part of that pleasant silence. The crowded place now looked desolated, with only a few people strolling around The Gate.

It was nearly ten when Aarav kept his hand on hers. "I think we should go", he said softly. She leaned her head against his shoulder, "it feels so good here", she said taking a deep breath.

"But you have a train to catch tomorrow."

"That's at three in the afternoon", she said.

"And what about dinner?"

"I can sacrifice my dinner for the sake of this beautiful night."

"But I can't", he laughed faintly, "you know, right now the only thing that's hitting my mind is your Maggi."

She raised her head, "You're feeling hungry?" she said, looking towards him. He nodded with a childish pout.

"Okay", she stood up, "let's go to my place, I'll cook it for you."

"No, I was just kidding", he smiled, "we can have dinner at any restaurant in Connaught Place, I can't trouble you anymore."

"Shut up", she said pulling him by his hands, but loosened her grip a second later and hit her forehead with her palm, "Oh! Shit! I don't have Maggi at my place", she said in her typical childish tone.

He laughed, "that's okay. Let's go to CP." She remained silent but almost yelled a couple of seconds later, "you have got some in your kitchen?"

He looked into her eyes. "Ya, but my flat must be a mess now, it's been closed for three weeks."

"So what, we will clean it, make Maggie and will watch a movie", she chirped.

"Okay", he said slowly. He felt delighted about getting some more time to spend with her.

***

"Look, it's as clean as a new one now", she smiled looking at him.

"Well it took almost an hour to make it so", he sighed, "and the entire energy." He sprawled on the sofa, "and see the monitor still looks dirty." She turned towards him making a face, "anything else sir", she asked sarcastically and moved towards the computer to clean it with the duster she had in her hand. He smiled, "and you too", he said and closed his eyes resting his head against the backrest of the sofa.

"yaa...", she stretched the word sadly, looking at herself, "my jeans and shirt, all ruined", she jerked her lips sideways, "I'm gonna have to take a shower", she turned towards him, "have you got something that I can use as night dress?"

"The wardrobe's all yours mam", he said, with his eyes still closed.

"I'm taking this big t-shirt", she said as she closed the wardrobe, "it's seems almost as long as my night gown", she laughed.

He opened an eye halfway, to see the t-shirt she picked, "sure", he said slowly and then closed it again.

***

The harsh sound of a falling utensil made him open his eyes. It took him a few seconds to gather himself, "are you in the kitchen?" He said loudly.

"Oh! I'm sorry", she came running into the room, "I woke you up", she said biting her lower lip, "actually it just fell off my hand", she showed him the sauce pan in her hand.

In the light green cotton t-shirt with her dark wet hair brushed down on a side to hang on one shoulder, she looked as beautiful as an artist's imagination. He gazed at her as if he was still dreaming, "wow! You look good", he said emphasising each word.

"Well, so can you, if you too take a bath", she said and walked back into the kitchen, "the water's really cold and refreshing", she added loudly.

He got down from the sofa and walked towards the kitchen, "You got the Maggi? It was inside the ... " he stopped as he saw the Maggi packets on the cooking shelf.

"Yup", she smiled, "it will hardly take fifteen minutes"

"Where's the towel?" he said.

"I left it in the bathroom."

"I'll be back in a jiffy," he said with a big smile on his face. She returned an even bigger smile.

***

"Yummm… that was amazing", he picked up the last noodle from his bowl and closed his eyes to cherish its taste.

Sitting on the sofa, with her legs curled up, she cast him a proud smile, "I have become an expert in cooking Maggi", she said. He opened his eyes, still in that delicious trance, "no doubt about it", he said and kept the bowl on the table in front of the sofa, "you deserve a chocolate", he added as he loosened himself on the cane chair that he had pulled in front of her.

"And when are you gonna get me that?"

"Right now", he smiled as he pointed towards his jeans hanging behind the door, "the one you gave me at the hospital, it is still there."

"Oh! God, how did I forget that?" She exclaimed as she stood up on the sofa to get it.

"I was just dying to have one", she said as she sat back with the Dairymilk in her hand, "it's like my medici…" she stopped, "Oh! Damn, hand it to me", she said pointing towards her hand bag lying on the bed behind him.

"What happened?" he frowned, while passing it to her.

"Your medicines, sir", she said, unzipping the bag, "here's the prescription and the medicines", she took them out of her bag. He made a face, "no, not today at least".

"Shut up", she said and gave him the bottle of syrup, "and these two before breakfast, this one in the afternoon before lunch…' she stopped upon noticing him gawking at her with his eyes wide open; totally perplexed.

She laughed, "it's not that tough to remember", she kept her hand on her mouth, still laughing, "okay I will write it down for you in simple language", she said and took out a pen and a piece of paper from her bag. Aarav moved himself to sit up straight on the chair and kept looking at her while she was writing.

"So, I have written their color and their tim … "

"Who's gonna do all this from tomorrow?" He interrupted her in a low cold voice that shook his own core. She looked at him for a while and then moved her eyes back towards the paper. *Why don't you say what I read in your eyes?* He wanted to yell out loud, but took a deep breath, *perhaps you don't want to or perhaps I'm reading my own confusion in there.*

"Got your packing done?" he asked, slowly wiping his face. She nodded, still looking into the paper, writing swiftly.

"At what time will you leave for the station, can I come to see you off?" He asked in a calm soft voice. She didn't answer and kept scribbling on the paper, but he could feel her breathing heavily. He remained silent for a while, "Ada", he sighed faintly, "are you gonna miss me?"

She stood up from the sofa with her face turned away from him, "I have to wash the sauce pan", she said blankly and sprinted towards the kitchen.

He pressed his temples and closed his eyes for a while. When he opened them back, his gaze fell on the paper that she had left on the table. He leaned in and picked it up. A soft smile floated across his face as he read it. "Yellow tablets-before breakfast, red ones-before lunch", his smile gradually broadened as he read the whole sheet.

While he was placing it back on the table, something written on the lower side of it caught his attention. He brought the paper close to his face and his eyes widened with surprise. He stood up from the chair and rushed himself towards the wardrobe. After a five minute struggle, he pulled out a brown woodland jacket from it, *yes, this is the one I was wearing that night*, he said slowly to himself and drowned his hand inside its inner pocket.

"Is this your name?" he said leaning against the kitchen door, with a thin smile on his face. She was hitting the tap over the sink with a palm and wiping her face with the other. She turned around, eyes swollen red, but she smiled. "What happened?" he said pointing towards her eyes. "Nothing, just touched them with the hand I cut onions with", she waved her hand in air with a just-forget-it look, "what were you saying?" She frowned slightly. He walked upto her and showed her the paper, "you have written something, is this your name?"

"Yaa", she smiled softly as she looked at it, "in Urdu, I learnt a bit when I was a child."

"And you love your name written in this language, right?"

She said, still smiling, "yaa".

"Well, that must be the reason you got this", he smiled and pulled out a bracelet from the pocket of his shorts. She kept both her hands on her mouth, "Oh! My God", she yelled, "so that muffler guy was you?"

He smiled, "so your hostel is in Chitranjan Park, midway between Kalkaji and Govindpuri and where is that kitten; still in your hostel?"

"She just ran away", she was unable to stop smiling. They kept looking at each other with huge grins on their faces. Suddenly, the tap made a strange sound and before they could move away, water rushed out through it and soaked them both, wet. Aarav quickly turned it off. "Damn! This bloody tap!" He said. They stood silent for a while and then burst into laughter. He looked at himself and then turned his eyes to her. His smile slowly disappeared, leaving behind a plain and silent appearance. He contemplated her face. The water droplets appeared to be some kind of shinning gems embedded on a fine piece of white marble and a few wet strands across looked like a graceful ancient art on it. He raised his hand slowly towards her face, her smile ceased with the movement. His dark brown eyes laid firm on her black ones, hearts pounding so hard they broke the pin drop silence of the room. He stroked her face with his finger, she half closed her eyes. His finger slipped down her face all the way from her forehead to eyes to cheek, like a feather falling under gravity. They clenched softly on her neck and drew her gently towards him. So close that he could feel her warm breath entangling with his own. He leaned slightly and as his lips touched hers, he felt her fingers seizing tightly on his shoulder and her flickering dark eyelashes now lay calm, covering the deep dark sea underneath it. He kept looking at her for a while and then pulled her closer and they melted down in each other like thirst and water.

***

148

He woke up only to find himself alone in the room. The killing silence around made him feel deserted on a far off island, amidst a calm ocean, stretched endlessly. It took him a few seconds to put himself together. He looked at the clock, which said '02:30 p.m.'. *She left!* he exclaimed inwardly, trying hard to catch up on his breath. He threw the sheet over his body and jumped off the bed. A fluttering piece of paper, on the table, grabbed his attention. He stopped, turned towards it and picked it up. It was a note Ada left for him which said, "It was nice meeting you Aarav, really nice. I'm taking the memories along—Ada." He felt choked and dried. He kept the paper back on the table and covered his face with both his hands. He wanted to yell at the top of his voice but could hardly feel any energy for it. He picked up his phone and dialed her number, "where are you?" He asked as soon as she received the call.

"At the station", she answered.

"I'm coming."

"No Aarav", she said loudly, "it's too crowded, you may get your ankle hurt and it's already 02:35 p.m., the train is about to arrive."

He took a deep breath, "I'm coming", he repeated firmly and disconnected the call.

***

The moment he entered the platform, Goa express whistled hard and moved with a jerk. He started running along with the slow moving train. "B6?" he held a porter by his shoulder and asked with all the nervousness in his voice. "Ahead", the porter said pointing in the direction of the train's movement. He ran in the indicated direction, but the accelerating train was threatening to outpace him. He ran faster, forgetting about the pain in his leg. He kept reading the numbers of the passing compartments; B3, B4, as he crossed B5, he saw her standing at the door of B6, half smiling, half crying.

"Why are you going?"

"Uncle, aunty, I have to take care of them", she replied in a shattered voice.
He looked into her wet eyes for a while, "don't go" he shook his head hard with his voice choking at every word.

Her eyes flooded with tears, "why?" She said slowly. He, like his eyes, was cold, being unable to answer the unexpected question. Her innocent face, all wet in tears seemed to plead for an answer. A part of the train had already moved ahead of the platform's end. *Why?* Her question echoed violently in his mind and he felt his lips trembling to answer it, but before he could, her compartment left the platform. He came to a halt and kept looking at her. She raised her hand and waved a bye, with smile on her face and tears in her eyes.

***

A sudden gush of wind gently struck his face and he opened his eyes. The stretched darkness, establishing the drowned sun, was as calm as it was twenty five years ago. He looked around, the flowers, swaying with the wind, looked extremely beautiful in the yellow flood lights and amidst them, with all the pride, the magnificent India Gate shone conspicuously. He took his cell out his pocket and looked at the time, 'five more minutes', he said with a mild smile on his face, 'just five more', he repeated his words in his mind. 'I have waited all through my life for this moment, just to see you again, to speak to you again', he took a deep breath, 'and to ask you the reason for not contacting me even once, all these years'. He covered his face with his palms, perhaps to control his emotions and wiped it hard.

A strong familiar scent filled his nostril, making him lose all his senses. His stomach cramped with the instinct of her arrival, heart beating at an unimaginable pace and blood ready to burst out his veins. He stood up from the bench and looked ahead. Like a streak of sunlight piercing through the floating clouds, she appeared, with a truly divine smile on her face, just as he had remembered it to be.

Lying on the bench, with his head in her lap, he gazed far into her wet beautiful eyes for hours. Not even a single question, out of those hundreds that he wanted to ask her, would form in his mind. He couldn't remember anything, feel anything, but her. He curled his fingers and touched her nose with his fist. Tears rolled down her cheek and fell on his face. Her soft hand reached out to his face to wipe it and then slid into his hair, caressing so softly that he couldn't resist closing his eyes.

***

"Sir, sir", a harsh male voice fell hard on his eardrums, making him open his eyes. "Sir, you can't sleep here", a uniformed guard, standing in front of him, said politely. He stood up from the bench and looked around as if he just came back from a different world. He swayed his eyes around, "was there someone else with me here?" He asked without looking at the guard. "No sir, I'm afraid there wasn't, is there anything I can help you with?" Aarav pressed his temples hard and closed his eyes, 'was it a dream? Why can't I remember anything clearly?'

"Sir, you need any help?" The guard interrupted his thought.

"Hah?" he turned towards the guard and it took him some time to comprehend his question,

"No thanks", he said and took out his cell. It was six in the morning. He looked around once again and then walked towards the main exit.

***

"Key for the room number 4215", he said weakly to the receptionist.

"Sir, you look stressed, do you need some medical assistance?" the receptionist enquired while handing him the keys.

"No thanks", he replied and headed towards the lift.

As he got out of the shower, he fell on his bed, his thoughts whirling like a tornado inside his mind. 'Did she actually come or was it just a projection of my strong urge to see her?' He tangled his fingers in his hair tightly, 'God! Why can't I remember anything clearly?' He said aloud and closed his eyes tightly, trying hard to remember. 'She kept her hand on my face and I fell asleep, but I was wide awake when she came'. He opened his eyes, upon a realization. 'Ya, that smell!' he said to himself and jumped off the bed towards the couch where he threw his clothes. He picked them up and smelled it. 'Yes, she came', his eyes widened, 'but why did you go away like this?' He said with a sad voice.

***

"Yes Mr. Khanna, how can I help you?" The receptionist on the phone asked.

"Could you please check the time for the next flight to Goa", he said, breathing heavily.

"Sure sir, just give me one minute", she said stressing on the word 'one'. He waited impatiently.

"Yes sir", she replied in less than half the time she had asked for, "next flight is at two in the afternoon." He looked at the wall clock, 'after five hours!' he exclaimed inside. "Alright book me a ticket for it then", he said.

"Sure sir, it will be delivered at your doorstep in a short while, 4215, right?"

"Yes."

"Anything else that I can help you with?"

"No, thanks", he said and hung up.

***

As soon as he got out of the Goa airport, he rushed towards the tourist inquiry centre in its premises. "Could you please get me the address for Westland library?"

"Sure sir", the guy on the other side of the counter said with a gentle smile, and snooped into his system. Aarav kept ticking his forefinger on the counter, with all the impatience in the world on his face.

"Sir, please write your name and cell phone number on this form and the address will be sent to you in a minute", the guy said. Aarav gave him an irritated look and pulled the paper towards himself.

"Where can I get a taxi?" Aarav asked, as he handed the paper back to the guy after jotting down the required details. The guy gestured towards the other end of the premises.

"Thank you", Aarav said without even looking at him and ran.

With his whole body shivering slightly and nerves aching as if stretched violently, he stood silently across the road, just opposite to the Westland library. He crossed the road and entered the small lawn in front of the library. He looked at the building and the lawn, worn out walls and dust all over the glass door and windows of the library, uneven grasses and weeds all around. Clearly it was much in need of maintenance. 'Perhaps it's closed or perhaps I've reached the wrong address', he thought and turned around to walk out. "Can I help you with something son?" A voice from behind stopped him. He whirled back. An old lady, perhaps in her seventies was standing at the glass door of the library, with some books in her hand and a soothing smile on her face.

He walked towards her, "Actually...I...I want to meet Ada", he swallowed hard, "I don't even know if she is still in Goa, we met in Delhi some twenty five years ba..."

"Aarav?" The old lady interrupted him in a trembling voice, "are you Aarav Khanna?" She exclaimed in her frail voice.

The change in the color of her eyes sent a wave of nervousness through his whole body yet his eyes widened with a streak of hope when she took his name. "Ye... yes", he said, in a voice as startled as his face. The lady took a good look at him, unmoved. He flung both his hands in the air, a second before the words came out of his mouth, "how come you know me, did she say something to you today?" His hurried voice and the expressions on his face were declaring his surprised state of mind out loud, "can you give me her home address, does she still live with her uncle and aun... ", his voice slipped into silence, all of a sudden and a thin smile accompanied the surprised colour, "you are her aunt", his smile stretched a bit. "Jenny aunty!!" he said loudly. She blinked firmly with a slight nod, "yes", she said slowly, "and she didn't say anything today, but I have seen your photographs in her notebooks and your face in her eyes for twenty five years", she added in a shattered voice.

He felt a thud deep down in his heart, "sorry?" He frowned.

She kept looking into his eyes for a while without saying a word and then turned around, pulling out a bunch of keys from her purse, "what made you come here after so many years?" She said while locking the door. "Actually aunty, she came to meet me at the India gate last night..." Her hands froze. The books and the keys in it fell onto the floor, sending a cascade of paper and metal clanking on the wooden floor, so loudly that it made him cringe. He bent down quickly to pick them up. "...and she just went away", he continued as he handed the books and keys back to her. She took them, still looking at the door. "That was a little strange, so I just thought to meet her once", he said.

She turned around to face him, old eyes brimming with tears, gleaming heavily from behind her specs, "did she meet you last night?" She said, with her hand on her mouth. The pain in her voice shattered his whole existence. Words didn't come out of his mouth that moment. He faintly nodded in reply.

She inhaled a deep breath and went as silent as a calm sea on a moonless night. "What's wrong?" He gathered all his strength to say that. "Could I meet her?" he added slowly. She took her specs off and wiped her tears, "you want to meet her?" she asked after some time, looking into his eyes, as she put her specs back on.

"Yes", he nodded.

"Come with me", she said firmly, as she walked ahead. He hesitated for a second with an unusual instinct thrusting inside him and then followed her.

***

There was no wind, every single leaf on the trees stayed unmoved, as if they had always been like this. The melting sun at the horizon was adding redness to the unidentified pain all around. He followed after her, but his mind was going insane with the hint of something that his pounding heart was not ready to accept at all. Leaving behind the civilization, some five hundred meters away, she stopped in front of a graveyard, after a long silent walk. His throat went dry. He found it so hard to breathe that his mouth fell open slightly for inhaling some air. She looked at him with watery eyes for a second before she pushed the gates. It made a loud creaky noise, which seemed even louder in the strange silence engulfing him. Wiping the tears in her eyes with one hand, she beckoned to him to follow her with the other. His fingers clenched hard in his palm to gather the strength against the deepening hint his mind was getting. He walked in. A little ahead, she stopped at a grave, the headstone quote of which was still not clear to him. He kept walking slowly towards the grave, and froze when he was able to read the inscriptions, which said, "In the loving memory of Ada Maciel: 14th February 1992- 17th June 2038."

He couldn't feel his body, it went numb as if every single drop of blood was drained out of it. He fell down on his knees and closed his eyes.

***

He didn't know which way he was going. He didn't know what time it was. The only thing he could see ahead was darkness and the only thing he could hear aloud were her words at the graveyard, still dinting hard at his mind and his soul. "She died of cancer, a week before the day she was waiting for since forever. She lived her whole life waiting for you to contact her, all she wanted was to meet you once, see you once."

*He had reached the end of the cliff. The ocean was shining in the silvery moon light. He looked down at the strong waves, a few hundred feet below; they made loud thunderous voice. He closed his eyes. Her last words at the graveyard echoed louder, "all through her life she kept saying it's not love, but the only name she took before dying was yours, what is it then... **if it's not love.**"*

Sweet, simple, passionate

strange, unusual, complicated

LOVE

sometimes is hard to understand

and sometimes really is

impossible.